COME FALL

"I'm getting us a water taxi," Sage said, his lips close to her ear, his warm breath caressing her skin. "After that, my love, I'm putting you to bed."

My love? She didn't dare make more of it than had been intended. "Bed sounds good," Vivianne murmured groggily.

Sage's arm circling her waist remained a steady anchor. She leaned into him, achingly aware of his hard body and the sensuous smell of a musky cologne. She'd never been so cared for, cherished, tended to. All this time she'd been starving for human affection; now she welcomed his touch.

Sage's voice was deceptively low when he whispered, "You'll tell me later what Vivianne Baxter is doing in Venice, alone."

The sound of her real name jolted her. "You know who I am?" Vivianne croaked, a sinking feeling in the pit of her stomach.

"I've heard a lot about Vivianne Baxter," Sage confirmed. "But I want to hear the real story."

She could only hope he would be open-minded. She badly needed a friend.

BOOK YOUR PLACE ON OUR WEBSITE AND MAKE THE ARABESQUE ROMANCE CONNECTION!

We've created a customized website just for our very special Arabesque readers, where you can get the inside scoop on everything that's going on with Arabesque romance novels.

When you come online, you'll have the exciting opportunity to:

- View covers of upcoming books
- Learn about our future publishing schedule (listed by publication month and author)
- Find out when your favorite authors will be visiting a city near you
- Search for and order backlist books
- Check out author bios and background information
- Send e-mail to your favorite authors
- Join us in weekly chats with authors, readers and other guests
- Get writing guidelines
- AND MUCH MORE!

Visit our website at
http://www.arabesquebooks.com

COME FALL

Marcia King-Gamble

BET Publications, LLC
http://www.bet.com
http://www.arabesquebooks.com

ARABESQUE BOOKS are published by

BET Publications, LLC
c/o BET BOOKS
One BET Plaza
1900 W Place NE
Washington, DC 20018-1211

All Kensington Titles, Imprints, and Distributed Lines are available at special quantity discounts for bulk purchases for sales promotion, premiums, fund-raising, and educational or institutional use. Special book excerpts or customized printings can also be created to fit specific needs. For details, write or phone the office of the Kensington special sales manager: Kensington Publishing Corp., 850 Third Avenue, New York, NY 10022, attn: Special Sales Department, Phone: 1-800-221-2647.

First Printing: July 2003
10 9 8 7 6 5 4 3 2 1

Printed in the United States of America

This book is for Vicki E, who wanted to be Valeria, but we settled on Vivianne instead. It is also for Emily, who has proven to be a wonderful friend and my right hand. Venice will always hold a special place in my heart.

ACKNOWLEDGMENTS

To Vicki Evinger, who encouraged me to write about Venice, and who thought Valeria was the perfect pseudonym for my heroine. I liked Vicki better.

To my critique group, fellow authors and wonderful Ya-Ya women. Thank you, Debbie St. Amand, Carol Stephenson, Victoria Marquez, Linda Anderson, and Sandra Madden. You simply are the best.

And finally, a great big thanks to my supportive editors, Karen Thomas and Chandra Sparks Taylor, for keeping me on track.

One

"God, it's beautiful. Looks just like a movie set." The overweight woman next to Vivianne gasped, wheezed loudly, then fanned herself with the map she was holding.

Although she said nothing, Vivianne agreed. St Mark's Square did look like a movie set. In fact, all of Venice did. No wonder it was called *La Serenissima,* "the most serene one."

Vivianne gazed around her, awed by the impressive Gothic and Byzantine architecture, home to the Pala d'Oro and the Museo di San Marco. Their tour guide had mentioned that the Basilica di San Marco was a must-see, and truly it was. She was amazed by the number of tourists wandering the square clutching bulging shopping bags, and the pigeons seemed to be everywhere. Some even pecked at her feet.

Venice. Hard to believe she was here. It was a dream come true.

Vivianne had traveled far to get to Venice and it had been worth it. Worth the money. Worth the long flight. Worth putting up with the excited, jabbering tourists.

A muscular arm whipped around her and she smelled the subtle scent of a musky cologne. Startled, she looked up into eyes that could only be described as smoldering coal. Of the twenty-five people composing their tour group, four of them were African American. He'd been hard to miss. He loped rather than walked, his confidence evident, and she'd avoided him like the plague.

"I assume you speak English?" he said.

Vivianne nodded. She couldn't speak. He'd literally knocked the breath out of her. She wondered where the young woman he was traveling with had disappeared to. She'd assumed they were a couple, although the age difference was very apparent. He had to be at least fifteen years older.

"Come on, you can do better than that," the man said, a twinkle appearing in his midnight eyes. "You've been much too quiet this entire trip."

He held out his hand. "I'm Sage Medino, and you're . . ."

Vivianne thought quickly. Telling him her real name would be disastrous and would probably cause him to turn away. She'd been labeled a hootchie mama and the world knew it.

"Victoria Barnard," she said, giving him the name she'd given everyone except her travel agent—unfortunately, her passport and documents couldn't be changed.

"Victoria, not Vicki?" One eyebrow arched upward and his mouth curved into a skeptical smile. "You look more like a Vicki to me."

Did he suspect Victoria wasn't her real name? The name Victoria had rolled off his tongue effortlessly and his gravelly voice made Victoria sound exotic and even Vicki sound sexy.

Vivianne wished he would stop staring at her and go find the young thing he'd been traveling with. She surveyed him from behind her dark glasses, taking in his well-muscled body, tight jeans, and form-fitting polo shirt with the trendy logo on his chest. Muscle-bound trouble.

Time to run.

She'd tried so hard to blend in with the crowd. She'd even downplayed her appearance, resorting to dark glasses and baggy clothes, hoping the disguise would shield her from curious glances and that she wouldn't be recognized for the notorious woman she was. So far it had worked.

"Please take your last snapshot," the Italian guide said, gathering them up, her practiced smile in place. "We're on a tight schedule and will need to move along." The yellow flag she held high above her head fluttered.

Sage's eyes scanned the area—searching for his girlfriend, Vivianne assumed. The young woman he'd been traveling with was nowhere in sight. "God, I dislike being herded. I'll catch up with you later," he muttered.

Good, he was leaving. Vivianne watched him stalk away. God, but he did have a nice butt. She wondered why if he hated tour groups so much he hadn't just come on his own. Surely he and his lover would be having a better time.

Vivianne had chosen Buena Vista Tours because it was one of the bigger travel consortiums in the United States. She had planned to get lost in the crowd. The company offered reasonable fares and attracted an eclectic mix of people, assuring her anonymity. She'd wanted to play tourist, and what better way to escape from the States and everything ugly it represented? She'd wanted to forget that Vivianne Baxter no longer had a job and that her life had turned into a nightmare.

So far so good. She'd managed to blend in with the crowd. Vivianne followed behind a couple who earlier in the trip had introduced themselves as Bonnie and Fred Edwards. They hailed from the Midwest and were having the time of their lives. They seemed unable to believe they had escaped the cornfields of Iowa and were now on a three-week jaunt through Europe.

Vivianne pinched herself. England had been exciting. She'd sailed down the Thames, gazed at Big Ben in awe, and seen the changing of the guards at Buckingham Palace. She'd even frequented the theater. Paris had been everything promised and more. She'd seen the Eiffel Tower, strolled down the Champs Elysées, and toured the Louvre. But Venice—Venice was special.

Vivianne breathed in the fragrances of a thousand scents. Freshly cut flowers mingled with the delectable smell of baked goods and the tangy aroma of ripe produce. There was even a nip in the air, which felt good. The group had taken gondolas to St. Mark's Square and she'd drooled over the couture clothing and attractive silk scarves in shop window. Stores nearby held beautifully made leather shoes and Murano glass pieces. She was dying to explore.

She spotted the back of Sage Medino's head, and grimaced. Even so, she used him as her beacon. He was certainly tall enough. He'd found the young woman, but didn't look too happy since she was busy chatting up the male student who spent most of his time sketching. The student was one of the four blacks on the tour and wore his hair in locks.

Their guide buzzed around, loudly counting heads, making sure they were all accounted for.

"Now we eat lunch, yes?" she said.

Vivianne placed one foot in the gondola. The handsome gondolier in his black-and-white-striped T-shirt and smart straw boater reached out to help her. Before she could take the large hand he offered, she felt a tug on her arm and jolted backward. The strap of her bag broke, and had it not been for a strong pair of arms steadying her, she would have fallen into the murky water. Vivianne straightened her sunglasses and leaned into her savior.

"Thank you." She felt for her purse. "Oh my God, I've been robbed. Stop the thief."

"Are you hurt?" Obsidian eyes scanned her face.

"I'm fine, but my purse isn't."

"Get into the gondola," Sage ordered.

Sage's powerful arms and legs pumped as he pursued the thief, who zipped by shoppers, pushing them aside. The man remained several paces ahead. He hopped into a speedboat and took off.

Vivianne froze. She was unable to move or make the smallest effort to get into the gondola. The people around her uttered words of comfort. Some tapped her shoulders; others offered the water they were carrying. What was she to do now? She had no bag and the little bit of money she'd carried was gone.

"He's gotten away," Fred Edwards cried excitedly.

"At least he didn't hurt you," Mrs. Edwards sympathized, taking Vivianne's arm and moving her off to the side. "Would you like some water, honey?"

"Call the police," her husband said to no one in particular. "Where's that damn tour guide?"

"I'm here." The guide, who was called Angelica, appeared wearing a worried expression on her face. "I've never had this happen. I've never had one of my tourists robbed."

"You have now. Find a policeman," Fred ordered. "A report should be taken."

No police. No report. Not if Vivianne could help it. She didn't need police snooping around asking nosy questions. There wasn't much in her purse to begin with, just a few lira, a guide book, and the postcards she had bought. She'd left her passport, jewelry, and travelers checks in the safe-deposit box back at the hotel. She did not need anyone knowing that Victoria Barnard was *the* Vivianne Baxter, spokesperson for the not-for-profit agency WOW, Women Off Welfare.

For the last few months Vivianne's face had been plastered on the front page of every American newspaper and tabloid. She had made headlines and been the topic of every television talk show, her face featured prominently in the news. She'd become the woman all women loved to hate.

Vivianne had been the director of public relations for

WOW. She'd spoken out on the importance of getting women on welfare back into the workforce, and making them productive, contributing members of society. She'd been well respected and lauded for her accomplishments. Overnight, all that had changed. She'd been accused of sexual harassment, and not just by one man but by several. The work she'd been so proud of had been reduced to nothing. The position she'd earned, it had been speculated, she'd gotten on her back.

Vivianne had survived the ensuing scandal. The case had eventually been thrown out. But her shame still remained. Who would have thought she would join the ranks of infamous women like Hill, Flowers, and Lewinski? She'd done nothing to deserve it, except for walking in on a conversation she never should have overheard.

"No. No police," Vivianne insisted as their tour guide frantically looked around for help. "I didn't have much in my purse and I would hate to hold everyone up."

"That might be so, but you can't just let a thief get away. He'll continue to rob unsuspecting tourists unless he is stopped," Fred Edwards said firmly.

Vivianne settled her sunglasses more firmly on her nose. "No harm done, really. I'm just a little shaken up."

All three peered at her incredulously. "You're just going to let him get away?" Fred said, shaking his head as if he were dealing with a lunatic.

Vivianne wished she could sink into her baggy shirt and disappear. She loathed the attention and just wanted to go back to being the unassuming tourist she had hoped to be when she signed up for this trip.

Sage Medino was back at her side. Sweat beaded his forehead and his coffee-colored skin gleamed with exertion. Even so, he smelled heavenly, a mixture of cologne and man.

"I didn't catch him," he gasped, panting heavily. "There

was an accomplice waiting. He hopped into a boat and took off."

"Thanks for trying," Vivianne said softly, touching his arm. "It was brave of you to chase the man. He could have been armed."

Sage managed a smile. His strong jaw jutted out. "I couldn't just let him get away."

A few lingering members of the tour group climbed into gondolas, shaking their heads. The women clutched their pocketbooks tightly.

"Such a shame," one muttered.

Angelica looked at Vivianne uncertainly. "Well, madam, what is it you would like me to do, fetch the police?"

"The group's waiting," Vivianne said.

"It would probably be wise for you to fill out a report," Sage cautioned.

"I'll think about it," she compromised. "Now if you don't mind I think I'll walk back to the hotel. You go on."

"I'm not leaving you alone," Sage said, scanning the horizon for the young woman accompanying him. She was seated in the gondola next to the male student with dreadlocks. She nodded sympathetically at them, then returned to her conversation. "Come on, let's walk," Sage said.

"I've already inconvenienced you. It's just a short way back to the hotel."

Vivianne wondered why he would so willingly abandon the young woman, who was chatting with the male student as if they'd known each other a lifetime. Maybe she had made a mistake. Maybe they weren't a couple after all.

Sage carefully assessed Vivianne as if he could see through her baggy shirt and inexpensive slacks. He stared at her as if he knew the dark glasses she wore were a prop. Did he suspect that she had cut her hair before the trip, and that the bangs peeking from under her straw hat had recently been colored a mousy brown to hide her auburn highlights?

Had he guessed that the eyes hidden behind her sunglasses had been skillfully covered by mud-brown contacts? The only thing she couldn't change was the teak of her skin.

"It's no trouble at all. It would be my pleasure to escort you." Sage took her elbow and steered her away from the group. "We'll catch up with you later," he said to the worried tour guide.

The young woman never even gave him a second look as he walked Vivianne away, leading her through picturesque cobblestoned streets and down a narrow alley. They crossed one of the four hundred bridges that spanned the city's one hundred and fifty canals, his hand remaining on Vivianne's arm. A strange tremor ran through her. The heat Sage gave off was comforting yet threatening. She felt as if she were a precious jewel that he had been commissioned to guard. His presence almost made her forget the awful thing that had happened. Only minutes ago she'd been robbed and violated.

Surrounding them were artists busy dabbing brushes into oils, their concentration focused on the canvases in front of them. Vivianne thought of her own amateurish renditions. She'd taken up painting as an outlet for her angst. It kept her hands busy and her mind blank. The last three months had been a nightmare. When you were unemployed you needed something to do other than reflect on your troubles. What would Sage think if he knew he'd come to the rescue of the infamous Vivianne Baxter? A woman with a tainted reputation.

Sage slowed down as they passed a crowd that had gathered. A mime, covered head to toe in silver paint, winked at them. The crowd applauded when he struck another pose.

"Oh, honey, isn't this wonderful?" an American-accented voice cried. "We've gotta get a photo of him."

The woman groped through her purse, successfully finding a throwaway camera.

Sage stepped forward. "I'd be glad to take a photo of you if you'd like."

The Americans smiled. "That would be great," the man said.

Vivianne watched them pose for the shot. She was still shaken up, but the golden sunlight soothed her. There was something about Venice, despite all the hustle and bustle, that made you feel peaceful and serene. She was determined to forget her troubles and simply enjoy. She would live for the moment. No one knew who she was and there were still several glorious weeks ahead. Why not live her dream?

"How about we get a picture of you two lovebirds?" the American woman asked, smiling brightly. Her camera was already posed.

Vivianne was about to correct the woman and tell her she and Sage were not a couple, when he interjected.

"That's kind of you—we left our camera back at the hotel," he said.

"Not a problem," the woman said cheerily. "Give us your address and we'll send you a copy of the photo."

Sage flashed the woman a dimpled grin and placed an arm around Vivianne. "Well, if you don't mind, thank you. Come on, smile for the camera, honey," he said, thrusting Vivianne up against his muscular body. She smelled the faint musky scent of man. *Okay, Vivianne, keep your cool, go with the flow.*

What the heck. Live for the moment, right? Let Sage worry about what to tell them when they asked for an address. She rested her head against his shoulder and smiled for the camera. The arm Sage had slung around her was taut and well muscled. He was used to taking charge.

After Sage thanked the couple and gave them his address, the couple wandered off into the crowd. The mime struck new poses and the crowd cheered and clapped. Several people tossed coins into the bucket at his feet. Eventually Sage took Vivianne's elbow and led her away.

"How about an espresso?" he asked after they'd walked several minutes in silence.

"Cappuccino sounds delightful," she answered, tossing him a rare smile.

"Cappuccino it is, then."

He led her into a nearby trattoria and waited until they were seated. "What does Vicki Barnard do when she is not playing tourist?" he asked.

Vivianne blinked at him. *Better make something up.*

"Well?" Sage prompted when she did not answer right away.

"I'm . . . uh . . . I'm . . ."

"Currently between jobs?"

"Yes, that's right. I'm looking for the right opportunity. What about you? What do you do?" Vivianne asked, hoping to switch his attention from her.

"I'm a consultant," Sage answered after a slight hesitation.

Vivianne peered at him from behind her dark glasses. "What type of consultant?"

He shrugged. "Securities. Any reason you're wearing your sunglasses indoors?"

"They're prescription," Vivianne snapped.

"I get the feeling we've met before."

"I assure you we haven't," Vivianne said firmly. "I have one of those faces like average Jane next door."

"There's nothing average about you. None of my next-door neighbors look like you."

"Thank you," she said, wondering if it was indeed a compliment.

A waiter appeared, another handsome olive-skinned Italian with white-on-white teeth.

"You are ready to order?" he asked, long, dark lashes batting flirtatiously at Vivianne.

Why would anyone be flirting with her? She'd worked so hard to be plain.

"We'll have a cappuccino and a double espresso," Sage answered, giving the waiter a searing stare.

"Right away, signor."

Vivianne arched an eyebrow at him. "Please, God, let me not be anywhere near you when that caffeine kicks in."

He threw his head back and roared. "You do have a sense of humor."

Vivianne remembered how he'd sprinted effortlessly after the thief, making it look as if he chased criminals every day of the week.

"Thank you again for coming to my rescue," she said, remembering her manners. "You will let me buy you dinner, it's the least I can do."

"I will, and I'll even let you pay the tip." Sage's long, ebony fingers splayed across the table. "In fact, I will let you do that this very evening. Our group has nothing planned."

"Seven o'clock, then, in the lobby?"

"Seven it is."

Why had she done that? She was flirting with trouble. Maybe she should have extended the dinner invitation to the woman he was traveling with as well. But he hadn't brought her up. Vivianne examined her nails. They were devoid of polish but were still long and well tended. Vanity had once driven her to a manicurist every week. Now she only did her toes.

"Are you using this vacation to sort out your life?" Sage probed.

"I guess you could say that."

"You're not very communicative, are you?"

Vivianne shrugged. Her life story would only make him run.

They were served their drinks. Vivianne took a tentative sip of her cappuccino. "Mmmm. This has got a distinct kick to it."

"Brewed the Venetian way," Sage said, gulping his own espresso before continuing in a deceptively calm voice, "What I don't understand, Vic, is why you were so reluctant to report the thief to the police."

Heat flooded Vivianne's cheeks. She bit back a smart-assed retort. Maybe she was just testy, angry at herself for getting robbed. He was only making conversation.

"There wasn't much in my bag to steal," she answered, tight-lipped. "Are you almost finished?"

She should pay but had no money. Not a great position to be in for someone accustomed to taking control.

Sage drained the last of his cup and tossed a handful of lira on the table. He came around to her side and offered a hand to help her up. Vivianne's annoyance ebbed as she walked with him to the exit. He seemed like a nice guy and she needed a friend.

"Ciao," their waiter called after them. "Buena Vista, bella."

"He likes you," Sage whispered. "So do I, even though you're not exactly forthcoming."

Vivianne grunted something unintelligible. She smiled and waved at the waiter, who winked at her. She'd not made herself unattractive enough. She'd make up for it tonight. Sage Medino would regret ever accepting her dinner invitation.

Two

Victoria Barnard fascinated Sage. Beneath her dowdy appearance was a sexy, vibrant woman, working hard to downplay her attractiveness. He planned on finding out why.

Sage had always had a good nose for mysteries. All of the men in his family had been in law enforcement. His father had been a cop, and so had his father's father. Most of his uncles were cops, some had even died in the line of duty. Sage had inherited a deep sense of honor. Truth and justice should prevail.

Vicki Barnard was working too hard not to stand out. She wore no makeup and her shapeless clothes had been deliberately selected. Even so, you couldn't help noticing her. She had what some women worked at all their lives but never achieved. Presence. She carried herself like a queen. Confidence permeated everything she did.

Sage had noticed her hands. The fingers were long, slender, and well groomed, a sharp contrast to the rest of her appearance. Why did she seem so familiar to him?

His FBI training had taught him to observe people and be vigilant in all situations. Those instincts had served him well all his life. Too well, or he would still be employed. His gut told him Vicki Barnard wasn't the unassuming plain Jane she appeared to be. She'd kept to herself from the very beginning and didn't seem interested in making friends. He'd never cared for flashy, loudmouthed women, and Vicki was certainly not that.

What bothered him was that she had refused to report the theft of her purse to the police. Why would any tourist choose to let a criminal get away? Most visitors in a foreign city would have been scared out of their wits to have something like that happen. Yet Vicki had chosen to let it go, and it didn't seem the logical thing to do.

Sage brushed an invisible speck of lint from the khaki trousers he had selected from his closet. This wasn't a date but there was no harm in looking his best. He glanced at his watch, realizing he had fifteen minutes to play with. Time to check up on Maya.

The phone rang as Sage patted his pants pocket, confirming that his wallet was there. He picked up the receiver. "Hello."

"Hey, haven't heard from you all day," a young female voice said.

Maya was on the other end. She'd beat him to it.

"What have you been up to?" he asked.

"I hung out with Alec. We had fun."

Alec was the young male student she'd befriended. They'd been introduced at the beginning of the tour.

"Do you have dinner plans?"

Maya chuckled. "Nothing definite. I'm considering staying in. How about you, what are you doing?"

That made him feel better. At least Maya would not be wandering the streets.

"I'm going out," Sage said.

"On a date?"

"Not a date, just grabbing a bite to eat."

Maya's laughter rang out. "And you weren't planning to invite me. Some friend you are."

Sage was in no position to invite Maya to dinner, not when he was a guest himself. He realized that Maya's plans to stay in might include Alec Randolf. The boy was not someone the Gabriels would approve of. They would have found his dreadlocks off-putting—plus, he clearly had no money. Sage's job was to keep opportunists at bay. But how much trouble could Maya get into left alone for a couple of hours?

"So, who are you having dinner with?" Maya wheedled. "Let me guess, it's that woman you were talking to earlier, the one whose purse was stolen?"

"That's none of your business."

"Hey, you can't always be the one asking questions."

She had a point.

"When will you be back?" she asked.

"Probably before midnight. Want to have coffee later?"

"Sure."

Sage refused to give in to guilt. Never mind that Nona and Stan Gabriel, Maya's parents, would have a cow if they knew that their precious daughter was left to the mercy of someone who looked like a reggae singer, and an unsuccessful one at that. Alec had worn the same baggy, raggedy jeans since the beginning of the trip, switching back and forth between three T-shirts in primary colors. He sometimes wore a baseball cap, the bill positioned backward on his head. Homeboy, Sage had labeled him. But someone as young and impressionable as Maya would find him attractive. To her he would be forbidden fruit. Lion-colored eyes sharply contrasted with a charcoal complexion and made him stand out. Two tiny gold earrings adorned each ear.

"You've got weird taste in women," Maya said. "I thought for sure that Kiana Lewis would be more your style."

Kiana was a divorcée traveling with the group. Her suggestive clothing indicated she was on the prowl, and she had made no secret of her availability or her willingness to accommodate.

"What do you know about my style?" Sage quipped. "I find Vicki Barnard both attractive and articulate."

"Different strokes for different folks," Maya said, laughing.

Sage joined in her laughter. He'd always enjoyed a challenge and Vicki Barnard would be one. Like any healthy, red-blooded male, he was intrigued. Besides, breaking bread with Vicki Barnard wasn't exactly the beginning of a lifelong commitment. He was convinced he knew her from somewhere and if he spent more time in her company it would eventually come to him. He never forgot a face.

"Differences are what make the world go around," Sage added. "What time do you want to meet?"

"Eleven-thirty at the coffee shop."

"I'll be there."

Sage hung up, thinking that Maya, charming child that she was, still focused on appearances, while he, with experience under his belt, knew there was a lot more to a person than that. He'd pretended to befriend Maya early in the trip, assisting her at the baggage carousel at the airport.

Maya had announced to her overprotective parents that she was off to Europe on her own, and movie stars Nona and Stan Gabriel had gone ballistic. Yet no amount of arguing could convince Maya to take a friend along. Her concerned parents had no choice but to acquiesce when she'd accused them of treating her like a prisoner and threatened to run off. They'd compromised by allowing her to join Buena Vista Tours. Sage had been hired as her bodyguard without her knowledge.

For someone not wishing to draw attention to herself, Maya's Louis Vuitton bags had been gigantic, weighed down with stuff. Stickers on the sides announced that she'd stayed at the Beverly Hills Hotel and other upscale resorts. Those stickers had given him just the opening he needed.

He'd introduced himself, stating that he too was from California. And so the bond had been formed.

At ten minutes to seven, Sage sauntered into the lobby and took a seat directly across from the elevator. He crossed one leg over the other and sank into one of the hotel's plush chairs. No sooner had he made himself comfortable than he was joined by Kiana Lewis. Tonight the divorcée wore a form-fitting, butt-hugging, red lycra dress.

"Waiting for someone?" She joined him in the adjacent seat and crossed one long leg over the other, letting him have plenty of thigh. High-heeled sandals encased pedicured feet.

"As a matter of fact, I am."

His rather abrupt retort didn't turn her off. Instead, her tongue rimmed ruby-red lips as she settled into the chair more comfortably. Kiana pouted those crimson lips at him. The color matched her toenails. "What a shame. I'd hoped you might join me for a cocktail at the bar."

"Some other time, maybe. We've got almost two weeks of touring left."

It was not in his nature to be rude to anyone. But Kiana didn't do it for him. He knew the type.

"Promise?" Kiana said, leaning over and placing a hand on his thigh, squeezing gently. Her full breasts almost sprang from a low-and-behold plunging neckline. Sage averted his eyes.

Thank God the elevator chimed. The doors swung open and Vicki Barnard emerged, her eyes scanning the immediate area, but missing him. She wore a shapeless black dress with a mandarin collar, and sandals on her pedicured feet. She had planted rimless spectacles on her nose and her short hair had been slicked back from a face devoid of makeup. Not even lipstick brightened up her coffee-colored skin.

Sage rose, intent on catching Vicki's eye.

"Here's my date," he said to Kiana.

Kiana sucked her teeth, dismissing Vicki as even a possibility. She stood and placed a lingering hand on his arm. "You're turning down drinks with me, for her?" She shook her head, clearly perplexed.

"Not turning down, just delaying our drink."

Sage was used to handling aggressive women. Even when he was married, women had come on to him. It had gotten worse since his divorce but now he knew what he didn't want. At age thirty-five he'd become selective about the women he dated. Kiana Lewis was not it. She was too predatory and spelled trouble.

"I'll catch you tomorrow," Sage said.

"I'd prefer it if you caught me now," Kiana hissed, storming across the lobby and heading for the bar.

Sage watched her disappearing back and shrugged. "Hi," he said, approaching Vicki. "You look nice."

She blinked at him from behind her owlish glasses and smoothed the shapeless black dress, clearly thrown by the compliment. He felt her whole body tighten when he took her elbow.

"Where are we off to?" he asked.

Vicki used her chin to indicate the concierge. "Let's ask him," she said in a cultured voice that he swore he'd heard some place before. "Concierges know all of the best places."

A woman obviously comfortable traveling. Vicki Barnard wasn't what she said she was, he'd bet.

They waited in line behind a Japanese couple. Sage approached the employee. "We're looking for a small, out-of-the way restaurant, any recommendations?"

"I'm sure we can find you something," The man began thumbing through a book. "Ah, yes, this will be perfect. It's not fancy, but the food is good and it is perfect for lovers."

Vicki looked like she wanted to disappear into her baggy dress. Sage noticed her feet; the hot-pink polish on her toenails was a strange contrast. The employee, oblivious to Vicki's discomfort, unfolded a map and proceeded to give them directions. "You can take a gondola or you can walk, whatever is your pleasure."

Sage looked to Vicki. "What will it be?"

"I feel like walking," she said. "It's a lovely night and it would be nice to stop and admire the wonderful architecture."

"Then walk we will." He extended his arm. She didn't seem to want to take it.

Sage squelched his disappointment. The thought of gliding through the canals in a gondola with Vicki, crumbling buildings surrounding them, had sounded like heaven to him. It would be nice not to have to listen to awed, chatty tourists yap on about souvenirs bought and bargains found.

"I haven't gotten much exercise since I've been here," Vicki said by way of explanation. "I want to take in the sights, sniff the smells, and touch the wonderful old buildings."

Liking her enthusiasm, Sage smiled. "Without fear of being herded, you mean?"

"Exactly."

"Large groups have a tendency to make me crazy," he admitted.

Vicki peered at him from behind her scholarly glasses. "I'm curious, why did you sign up for a tour if you hate being on a schedule and dislike being herded?"

"Because it was the only affordable way to get to Europe."

Sage had no way of knowing how she would react if he told her that the money he'd been offered by Stan and Nona Gabriel was too good to turn down. He'd been hired to shadow the movie stars' daughter and he needed a salary to live. Getting a job with the Gabriels had been a godsend. His career was in shambles, and all because of an envious colleague.

"The price was certainly right," Vicki said, not giving him

the third degree as he'd expected. She pointed to a fleet of boats on the Grand Canal lit up with colorful lights. Drunken Venetians hung off the sides, smiling and calling to them, wine flowing freely. "What's going on?"

"Probably another festival. The Venetians love their festivals."

Sage placed his hand at the small of her back, steering her through almost empty streets. He was surprised when she let him. They stopped occasionally to peer into store windows or glance at the map. It was too early for Venetians to have dinner and after a day or so in Venice, most tourists followed the pattern.

Mangare, their restaurant, was set back from the road. Little more than a hole in the wall, it had room for about twelve couples. An affable waiter led them to a table for two at the back and seated them behind an ornate screen.

"You will want to be alone," he announced, making sure the folding screen was adjusted to allow sufficient privacy but still give them an unobstructed view of the other patrons.

The man had mistaken them for a couple. The idea wasn't off-putting, though Vicki wasn't his normal type. She was certainly nothing like his ex, Lisette, a glamorous, vain creature who was an overachiever. One day she'd packed up her things and left him. Later he'd learned she'd been having an affair with her boss. Her deceit had left him wary and distrustful of women in general, especially those in the corporate world.

Sage held out Vicki's chair and waited for her to sit.

"Would you like the house wine or should I get you a wine list?" their waiter asked.

Sage raised an eyebrow and looked to his companion. He didn't even know if she drank.

"The house Chianti is fine with me," Vicki said, taking charge. "Is that okay with you?"

She was no shy retiring wallflower, that was for sure. Sage put the finger on why he was interested in her. He sensed that under the surface lay a complex woman. He loved mysteries and was drawn to solving problems. That was what had made him the ideal FBI agent.

Their waiter returned with a basket of crisp rolls covered with a plaid cloth. A carafe of Chianti and two glasses followed. When the man was through pouring, he said, "I'll leave you to look at the menu. You can't go wrong with any of our specials."

After he left them, Vicki looked around and sighed contentedly. "This was the perfect choice. No noisy crowds. No tourists demanding hamburgers. It feels good to relax."

And relaxed he was, surprisingly. He clinked his glass against hers. "Here's to getting to know you."

Vicki averted her gaze. Sage wondered why she suddenly appeared uncomfortable. "I'd like to know all there is to know about Vicki Barnard," he continued

"There's not much to tell," she said, still not looking at him. She selected a roll from the basket and began munching on it. "As I mentioned before, I'm just Jane average."

He doubted that. "Okay, whatever you say. What did Jane average do when she had a job?"

Vicki's expression became guarded. "Wrote speeches," she said, almost reluctantly.

"Interesting. I bet you were good at it."

"So I've been told."

He loved her voice. Polished and sexy, contrasting strangely with her outward appearance, which was bland.

"Were you an English major?"

"Sociology."

Sage raised a quizzical eyebrow. "Social work is a thankless job and pays nothing, I've heard."

"Money isn't everything," she said, crumbling a roll between well-tended fingers. "It's rewarding hard work and you do make a difference in people's lives."

Vicki's tone indicated she believed what she said. She

now gave him her full attention. Her gold-flecked eyes through the lenses of the disfiguring glasses gleamed with intensity. She was passionate about helping people and genuinely cared about those less fortunate. He was intrigued.

"What about you? Tell me about your security business," she said, nibbling on her roll.

Sage drummed his fingers against the table. Security business? What security business? Oh, yes, his little white lie. "My company provides guards for hire," he fabricated.

"Sort of like Pinkerton."

Sharp as a tack.

"Exactly."

Sage reached over and took her hand, squeezing gently. Vicki tugged it away as if he had scorched her, and began searching the menu. "The Portobello mushrooms sound delicious and I'll have the penne," she babbled. "Be right back. I need to use the ladies' room."

Vicki picked up her purse and rushed off. He liked the slight sway of her hips under the bulky dress. She had deliberately chosen the drab black dress, he would bet. Even so, her womanly figure could not be ignored. He dismissed the sharp tug in his loins, putting it down to being celibate for too long.

The restaurant began filling up with locals. Waiters greeted families with hugs and kisses as if they were best friends. Sage caught their waiter's eye and called him over.

"The lady wants the Portobello mushrooms and I'll have the calamari."

"Excellent choices, signor."

Vicki was taking a long time. Too long. Sage sipped his Chianti and sat back in his chair, his attention focused on four men who were huddled around a table. They didn't seem the type for a family-style restaurant and looked totally out of place. He pictured them patronizing a fast food eatery, slugging down beer, and ogling the women. Another five minutes went by. He focused on the cream-colored walls and the alabaster statues that were part of the decor.

Vicki returned clutching a stained envelope. She had visibly aged. Sage was up like a shot. "What's wrong? Are you ill?" he asked, pulling out a chair and practically shoving her into it.

"This note was placed under my stall."

Sage pried the envelope from between her stiff fingers. He opened it and read the message.

We know where you are. No point in hiding.

"Breathe deeply," he ordered.

Vicki sat and did as he said.

"Have some water," he said, handing her a glass.

Vicki gulped down half the liquid.

"Now," Sage said, "suppose you tell me what's going on. Start at the beginning."

Vicki Barnard stared at him from behind her owlish glasses.

She was in shock, he decided. Sage scooted a chair next to her and gave her his hand. Vicki held on to it like a lifeline and after a while said, "Nothing's going on. At least nothing you need to be involved in."

He persisted. "Are you in some kind of trouble?"

"Not anymore."

Her cryptic responses were beginning to annoy the heck out of him.

"Look, I can help you," he said. "I'm good at keeping confidences."

The hand he was holding returned to her lap. "I can fight my own battles, thank you."

He bet she could. But she would fight them better with a helping hand. And who better to help than an ex–FBI agent?

Three

"Oh, Alec, I'm having the best time," Maya said, sucking down another of the colorful drinks Alec handed her. She gazed about the noisy nightclub, unable to believe that she was on her own with no parents watching her. She could do anything she wanted.

"Cool," Alec said. "I'm glad you're enjoying yourself, I knew you would." He bopped to the pulsating beat and gulped his beer in several quick swallows.

Alec Randolf was different from any of the men Maya Gabriel knew. He fascinated her and was such a contrast to the superficial sons of her parents' friends whom she was forced to date. He was impulsive, outspoken, and in many ways unpolished. And he was showing her such a different world.

Onstage, a punky, androgynous type with dyed blond hair and dark roots belted out the words of a rap song. The music booming from the speakers was loud and frenetic, nearly drowning out Alec's words. It was still early, but the nightclub was packed with a funky mix of young people and getting fuller by the minute.

"Want to dance?" Alec asked, taking Maya's drink just as the music switched to a popular hip-hop tune.

He didn't wait for an answer, just set down his empty beer bottle and the glass on a nearby table. He grabbed her hand

and together they pushed their way onto the crowded dance floor.

Sweat poured off the dancers, and the smell of beer and hard liquor couldn't be missed. They squeezed into a spot barely large enough to hold two people. Alec immediately threw his hands in the air and began wiggling his hips. He gestured for Maya to come closer, his hips doing most of the talking. Alec's bulging biceps, strong neck, and spectacular face drew a lot of attention. He'd told Maya he worked construction part-time to help put himself through college. Boy, did it show.

The alcohol was still warm in Maya's belly and made her feel daring. She gyrated her hips and undulated her pelvis, matching him move for move. She wanted him to notice her, and not just as a friend. Alec didn't disappoint her; his hungry gaze swept her body but he didn't miss a beat.

"Wow, it's hot," he mouthed, yanking off his T-shirt and tying it around his waist.

Maya couldn't help staring at him. She moistened her lips and let her eyes trail downward. Sweat glistened from Alec's well-defined pectorals and streamed down his chest, settling in his belly button. He threw an arm around her neck, bringing her up against the lean hard length of him. She could feel every sinewy muscle, even the thump of his heart. The heat coming from his skin seared her. The beginnings of an erection pressed into her center. She was enjoying herself as she never had before.

No one in Venice had ever heard of Maya Gabriel, and if they had, they didn't care. That she was the daughter of two famous movie stars was irrelevant. She was free to behave like any normal young person. She didn't have to watch to see if a photographer had stalked her, or worry about whether her photo would appear on the front cover of a trashy tabloid. Freedom felt good.

An illuminated clock on the wall flashed the hour. Eleven

o'clock. Where was she supposed to be at eleven-thirty? It didn't matter, not when she was having so much fun. The girl dancing next to Maya bumped into her. Alec tightened his hold around her waist.

"Steady now," he said, the look in his eyes sending shivers skittering down her spine. "Having fun?"

Maya nodded. "Oh, yeah. This place is slamming." Slamming was an expression she'd picked up from him.

"Let's get another drink," he said, leading her off the dance floor and toward one of the crowded bars.

When he put his T-shirt back on, Maya felt a rush of disappointment. She'd enjoyed having a full view of his naked skin. Alec winked at her and flicked auburn-colored dreadlocks off his face. His cheekbones were high and slanted. Most women would die for them. Maya followed his broad back as he pushed his way past skimpily clad young women whose tongues practically hung to the ground, eyeing him. Alec carried himself like a god, head held high, amber eyes scanning the periphery of the room.

Maya's steps faltered. She remembered where she was supposed to be. She'd promised to meet Sage for a drink. Longing to stay with Alec and at the same time feeling obligated to Sage, she nibbled her lip. What to do?

"What's up?" Alec asked, tossing her a tawny-eyed glance over his shoulder. "Why are you stressing?"

Was it that obvious? Maya shouted over the music, "Not stressing. I've got to leave in a few minutes. I promised Sage I would meet him."

"Sage? You mean that old guy who keeps hanging around you?"

Maya chuckled. "That's Sage. He's hardly old and he doesn't hang around me. He looks out for me."

She wasn't about to tell him that she was flattered by Sage's attention. And in fact thought he was cute.

Alec grunted. "Keep fooling yourself, girlfriend. The man's got the hots for you."

"No, he doesn't," Maya protested. "We're both from L.A. and that creates a bond."

One eyebrow rose imperiously. "If you say so."

While they waited for the bartender to serve them, Alec draped an arm around Maya's shoulders. She leaned into him, inhaling his musky male scent. He made her feel both safe and free. A bevy of underdressed females paraded by but Alec didn't even glance their way. Impulsively, Maya kissed his cheek and felt him stiffen. What was the problem? Wasn't he attracted to her?

She had to go. She wouldn't feel good standing Sage up. He'd been wonderful company until she'd met Alec. But Alec was closer to her age and so much fun, with his street-smart ways and outrageous attitude. He was twenty-two, two years her senior, and he'd lived a life she'd never known.

Alec ordered their drinks; a bottle of beer for himself and a colorful concoction for her. Maya sipped the heady drink. She was already tipsy, and the light-headed feeling the liquid produced made her feel carefree and open to the possibilities. Except she didn't have time to explore possibilities. She needed to leave.

The music changed to a slow tune. "Let's dance," Alec said. He didn't wait for an answer, simply grabbed her hand and guided her onto the dance floor.

Despite knowing that she would probably not complete the set, she laid her head on his shoulder and rubbed her cheek against his woolly dreadlocks. Destiny's Child played on as Alec's arms circled her waist, his fingers lightly massaging the base of her spine. God, it felt good to be held in his arms as he began a slow agonizing grind.

Alec was special, not full of himself like the guys she was forced to date. He listened when she spoke and his conversation wasn't peppered with tales of grandiose achievements.

She knew her parents would disapprove of him. They would consider him out of her league, not fit to polish the strappy sandals she wore. But her parents were not here and their opinion didn't count. Not here in Venice.

Sage waited at the hotel's coffee shop for Maya to show up. She was already fifteen minutes late and he was getting worried. What if something had happened to her? He should never have let her out of his sight, and all because of some bizarre interest in Vicki Barnard. Time to get his priorities straight.

Thinking of Vicki brought to mind how the evening had ended. She'd been adamant about not going to the police and Sage had given up convincing her. He'd seen Vicki to her door, made sure the safety lock clicked into place, and then gone to meet Maya. He hoped Vicki was asleep by now. She'd tried to cover it up, but she'd been badly shaken by the note shoved under that bathroom stall. If Vicki was just an ordinary somebody, no one would be threatening her. Average Janes did not receive threats.

Sage had searched the restaurant looking for anyone suspicious. He'd even snuck into the ladies' room and examined every nook and cranny. His perusal of that area had only served to scare an old lady busy adjusting her girdle. She'd screamed so loudly that Sage thought the entire restaurant had heard her. But no one had come to investigate and he'd returned to their table, giving the patrons a quick once-over. They all seemed normal, just people from the neighborhood out having a good time. The four men seated at the table had left.

But someone had deliberately followed Vicki Barnard to Mangare's, and someone had slipped her that note.

Ten minutes went by. Sage ordered another espresso, hoping to God that Maya was safe. He would give her approximately five minutes, and then he was heading to reception to call her, just as he'd done when he first arrived.

A group of young men entered the coffee shop, chattering loudly in Italian. They sat at one of the banquettes and placed their orders. Sage didn't speak a word of Italian and didn't know what they were saying. He glanced at his watch. Damn Maya for being so irresponsible. He never should have let her out of his sight.

A couple sauntered in, people he recognized from the tour group. They nodded at him before taking seats at the table next to him. A muted television featured world news on the only English station. From his location Sage could not hear the newscaster but could clearly read the subtitles. An American politician held court expounding on a national disaster in Kansas. When he was through the newscaster came on again. Sage focused on the subtitles. Vivianne Baxter, the ex-spokesperson for WOW, Women Off Welfare, was missing.

There was a closeup shot of an attractive woman in dark glasses hurrying from a courtroom. She vaguely reminded him of someone. Sage recalled the scandal. It had made headlines. For a while there Vivianne Baxter had become a recognizable face, an ordinary woman who overnight had become infamous.

It really was a shame. The Baxter woman had been a role model, championing the cause of underprivileged females and working hard to assimilate them back into the workforce. Although Sage wasn't big on career-driven women, he admired her spunk. Vivianne's name might have been cleared but to many she was still a fallen woman. He didn't know what to believe, but he knew what it felt like to be set up.

Sage had followed the scandal for a while, his sympathies with Vivianne. He'd been a well-respected FBI agent with ten years on the force, cited for extraordinary deeds of heroism and slated for a director's slot. He'd enjoyed an exemplary work record up until a few months ago, before his whole world had come tumbling down around him.

He and his buddies had made one of the largest cocaine busts in history. They'd been lauded for this feat until the evidence disappeared. Then Sage had been accused of stealing the coke and using it for his personal gain. Any denial of wrongdoing had fallen on deaf ears. Since he was the last person in the evidence room, circumstances seemed to point to him. First he'd been suspended pending investigation, then forced to resign.

Maya came rushing in just as Sage was beginning to relive his ordeal. She was all wild-eyed and flushed. Her hair fanned her face and the men at a nearby table sat up whispering softly in Italian. It didn't take a rocket scientist to figure out what they were saying. Maya was being eyed as if she were more delicious than the cannoli they gobbled. One of them said something, but Maya ignored him. There was no sign of Alec. Thank God.

"Hey," Maya said. "Sorry I'm late." She slid into the seat across from him, smiling beguilingly. "You're not mad, are you?"

Sage made a production of looking at his watch. He refused to cut her slack. "Should I be? As I recall, you were supposed to be here forty-five minutes ago, and you did say you were staying in."

"Where's your date?" Maya asked, totally nonplussed. She twirled her hair, flirting with him.

"In bed. Where's yours?"

"Who said I had one?"

Coy. A handful. Used to getting lots of attention.

"Just a guess." Sage refused to be drawn in to her flirting.

"Alec and I went to a nightclub, if you must know."

"Nightclub?" Sage knew he sounded horrified. "And John Travolta didn't come back with you?"

"He remained at the club."

"Some gentleman."

"He put me in a taxi."

Sage narrowed his eyes. "You didn't tell me you were going to a nightclub."

"Hey," Maya said, tossing a mop of curly hair out of her eyes. "I changed my mind. You know, you're starting to sound like my father and you're ticking me off."

Sage supposed he did. But Maya's father, Stan, had entrusted him with her care. If Sage had known the girl's plans involved a nightclub he would never have gone to dinner with Vicki.

"So tell me about your date," Maya said. "Was it fun?"

"It wasn't a date. Vicki and I simply had dinner. She wanted to thank me for coming to her rescue earlier today."

"I bet she did." Maya looked at him skeptically. "She reminds me of someone. I just can't think who."

"She does seem familiar. Do you want something to drink or maybe dessert?"

His precocious charge shook her head, tangled ringlets bobbing. "No, thanks. I've had plenty to drink."

"I've noticed," Sage said. "And you're not even twenty-one."

Maya wrinkled her nose. "There's no legal drinking age here in Italy."

"A pity."

"God," she cried. "I thought I had left my dad back at home in the States. I'm not by any means drunk."

Safer to change the topic. Much as he hated the job of following some spoiled little rich kid around, he happened to like Maya. Keeping her in sight would be much easier if he stayed on her good side.

"What are your plans tomorrow?" Sage asked.

Maya twisted a lock of wiry hair and grimaced. "I'm not doing the group breakfast if that's what you're asking. I hate being forced to sit with all those people yakking about nothing. Alec and I are having coffee at the outdoor café down the street. We'll decide then what we want to do."

Boy, was she bent on making his life hell. If he wanted to keep her in sight, he would have to invite himself along.

"No museum?" Sage asked.

The group would be heading for a museum in the morning and an outdoor concert after lunch. The rest of the day was free for shopping or sight-seeing.

"No museum. I'm sick of a crowd. Alec and I want to spend quiet time together so we can get to know each other."

"That's not a good idea."

Maya slapped both hands on the table, making several heads turn. "What is it with you? I'm not running off with the guy. I just want to spend time with someone closer to my age. Someone who's fun."

Time to lighten up. "I'm not fun?" he asked.

"You can be when you're not playing a parental role or acting like you own me." Maya batted her eyes at him. "Alec thinks you have the hots for me and I . . . well, I think . . . sheesh, I don't know what to think."

"How about you think that I'm looking out for you? Just one Californian looking out for another Californian. I wouldn't want to see you get into trouble."

"Is it that you don't like Alec?" Maya said, getting to the point. She stood, poised and ready for flight. "Do his dreadlocks turn you off? I happen to like the look. He's funny, funky, and totally comfortable with himself. Sure, he's unconventional, but that's what makes him unique. He's not like the rest of this group, always talking about their money and the things that they have."

"Alec's dreadlocks have nothing to do with it. I'm concerned that you're an impressionable young woman and I don't want him turning your head," Sage snapped.

"There you go playing my father again," Maya stormed. "I came on this trip to have fun. I deserve some. If you want to remain my friend, then you're just going to have to lighten up."

Sage got up and grabbed her arm. Maya jerked away from him. "Take your hands off me."

People were starting to stare.

"Look, I'm sorry," Sage said, trying for a more conciliatory tone. "I overstepped my bounds. You're a big girl. I'm just asking that you be careful."

"I am careful. Have a good night. I'll see you tomorrow."

"Maybe I'll join you for breakfast and get to know Alec and see just how wonderful he is?"

Maya glared at him before hustling off. "I'll discuss it with Alec and see what he thinks."

"Till tomorrow, then," Sage called after her.

She didn't turn back.

Even so, Sage planned on being at the café for breakfast. He knew the perfect person to take along. He would invite Vicki to breakfast. *Not Vicki, Vivianne Baxter.*

The realization of his discovery propelled him out of his chair. He'd finally placed the face.

Four

We know where you are. No point in hiding. The words replayed themselves in Vivianne's head as she sat on the outdoor patio of a local café sipping a cappuccino. Maybe, just maybe, the note hadn't been meant for her.

Sage had asked her to breakfast. After enduring another sleepless night, worrying, breakfast was supposed to have been a relaxing affair. Only it had come as a surprise to find Alec and Maya seated under a colorful umbrella. Sage had immediately taken it upon himself to join them.

Alec looked none too pleased at the invasion, but managed, "Sure, sit down." Since then he answered their questions with one-word sentences and continued wolfing his breakfast while Maya toyed with her fruit. The meal was turning out to be a tense affair with the two men verbally sparring with each other.

"So, what are your plans today?" Sage asked the young people.

Alec shrugged. "We're planning to hang."

It was the longest sentence he'd strung together.

"Does that mean you're skipping the museum?" Sage's long fingers reached for a roll.

"Yep. I hate organized tours; I'd rather go to the museum on my own."

"If you hate organized tours so much, why did you sign up for this one?"

Sage was virtually repeating the same questions she'd asked him.

"Because it was affordable," Alec snapped. "I wanted to see Europe and this was a way to do it."

Voice dripping with sarcasm, Sage responded, "So you think you would benefit more by reading from some guide book and wandering Venice on your own?"

Alec set down his knife and fork. "We have no interest in getting off a bus and following a bunch of middle-aged tourists and senior citizens up and down steps. Right, Maya?"

She nodded and gave him an adoring look.

"Okay, okay, we'll join you," Sage said, looking directly at Maya and making her squirm.

"Yes, I suppose that would be fun," the girl said half-heartedly.

Alec didn't argue but his expression said it all. He wanted them the hell out of there.

What was it with these two men vying for the young woman's attention? And why did she feel like a pawn? Vivianne tamped down her annoyance. She'd had enough. Digging into her purse, she found lira and tossed the bills on the table.

"Well, folks, it's been nice having breakfast with you," she said. "I'm going to catch the bus and join the middle-aged crowd."

Sage's arm whipped out, staying her departure. He gave the lira back. "I'll take you to the museum another time if you'd like. Play hooky, let's join Alec and Maya."

"Let's not invite ourselves where we're not wanted."

Alec's mouth opened and closed. Before he could say another word, an embarrassed Maya interjected, "Oh, yes, Vicki, come with us. We'll get a chance to chat."

Vivianne was torn. She'd been looking forward to the museum. On the other hand, she liked the idea of spending time with Sage.

"What do you say, Sage?" she heard herself ask.

"I say, yes, you absolutely should come."

Why not? It would be nice not to be on some crazy schedule, to wander aimlessly and see another side of Venice and hopefully Sage. *Easy, Vivianne, you don't need to become too attached. You already have enough trouble.*

She decided to ignore Alec's obvious annoyance. If he would rather have Maya to himself, he should have spoken up. Vivianne relished the presence of people. She'd had two scary things happen in a relatively short time, and she was shook-up. Why would someone have followed her to Venice, and why would they threaten her? Her case had been dismissed. She had lost her job. What would anyone want with her?

The last few months had been unpleasant. After being wrongfully accused of sexual harassment, she'd been virtually ostracized. Her supposed friends had turned their backs on her, even the woman she'd so admired, her boss and mentor Kathryn Samuels, had been convinced she was guilty. Board members like Juan Fernandez and Carl Daniels, men who'd been her biggest allies and staunchest supporters, had never once spoken up in her defense. Only her family had believed her.

"Okay, that's settled then. What are we going to do?" Sage asked, signaling the waiter for their check.

"I want to go shopping," Maya piped up. "And I don't want to go to tourist places. I want to go where the Venetians go."

"We'll ask the concierge for suggestions," Sage said, wrestling Alec for the check and paying the bill when it arrived.

A half hour later, they set out on foot to catch one of the public ferries. The little depot was nothing more than a run-down shack where an eclectic assortment of people were gathered. Tired-looking women clutched shopping bags, and storekeepers on their way to work jostled for position. As the vaporetto came into sight, elderly locals emitted impatient sighs. They purchased tickets and got aboard the crowded ferry, watching the young couple surge ahead.

Alec placed an arm around Maya, holding her steady. She wore a bright smile and leaned into him, totally captivated by what he was saying. For a fleeting moment, Vivianne envied them their youth and carefree attitude. What she wouldn't do to turn back the clock. She'd always been the type of person who made physical contact with the people she befriended, a hug here, a kiss on the cheek, a touch on the arm. That touchy-feeliness had gotten her into trouble.

At any other time this ride would be fun. She would have looked forward to exploring every nook and cranny of Venice. But life had a funny way of playing cruel tricks on you; today she just needed to keep busy.

Something inside her had died and now her perfect world wasn't so perfect anymore. Who could hate her so much? What had she stumbled onto that made someone feel threatened?

"Hey," Sage said, breaking into her musings. "What's going on in that pretty head of yours?"

Pretty? She no longer thought of herself as pretty. If anything, she'd done everything to downplay her looks. Even today, she'd opted for black baggy pants and an equally shapeless T-shirt. The one spot of color was her pink straw hat with the brim dipped artfully over one eye. And she'd kept her sunglasses on. She needed to.

Sage placed a finger beneath her chin and tilted her face upward. "I just gave you a compliment. The polite thing to do would be to say thank you." Where he touched her, burned.

"Thank you, but I hardly consider myself pretty."

"I beg to differ."

Another hot flash. The overcrowded ferry had nothing to do with the warm feeling that suffused her. She was grateful when the boat pulled into a berth and they were pushed and shoved from either side as people got off.

"Is this our stop?" she asked Sage.

"Beats me. Let's ask Maya and Alec," he said, grabbing her hand and tugging her through the milling crowd.

Alec looked none too pleased when they approached them.

"Yeah, I think this is where we get off," he said, consulting the map the concierge had given him.

They leaped off the vaporetto seconds before the boat pulled out again. Following a narrow street leading to one of many bridges, they crossed one piazza and then another. A maze of small alleyways lay ahead.

Sage flipped a coin. "Heads, we go right. Tails, left."

"You go right and we go left," Alec said rudely.

Sage ignored him. He was holding on to Vivianne's hand and she was letting him. She was getting the uneasy feeling that she was being shadowed and she couldn't quite say why. It was as if eyes bored into her back, but every time she turned around no one seemed to be paying the least bit of attention to them.

A group of men sat smoking cigarettes and guzzling espressos on the sidewalk. Maya skipped ahead, excitedly pointing out the cool clothes on the mannequins in the shop windows. They trudged up streets with names like Calle San Antonio and Calle Bondi, past pizzerias and tiny grocery stores. Inside, locals squeezed produce and screamed to each other in excited Italian. Outside, elderly ladies dressed head to toe in black took measured steps, heading for some unknown address.

Street musicians and artists plied their craft on every corner. Alec, entranced by the scene, loosened up. He appeared less sullen when he stopped to gaze at a canvas and comment on the artist's work. Maya hung on to his every word; her crush was in full bloom.

An hour later, Vivianne still could not shake the feeling that she was being followed. She glanced surreptitiously over her shoulder and swore she saw a shadow move. Probably just her imagination. Sage still had hold of her hand. He frowned at her.

"Why do you keep glancing over your shoulder?" he asked. "Are you shaken up by last evening's events?"

"Maybe a little," she admitted.

"It's not too late to go to the police. You've had two pretty bad scares in a short space of time. You've been targeted by someone."

Vivianne shook her head. "If it happens again I'll consider it. Right now I just want to wander aimlessly and drink in the sights."

If she went to the police she'd have to tell them who she was. She'd have to show identification and be forced to relive her nightmare. Time to put that part of her life behind her.

They stopped in front of a little church with a beautiful Gothic steeple. Alec took a seat on the steps and whipped out a sketch pad. Maya hung over his shoulder watching his deft strokes come to life.

"I'd like to go in," Vivianne said, her voice a mere whisper.

"I'll join you," Sage answered, his arm now around her waist. He glanced at the young couple and seemed to come to a decision.

Fascinated by the ornate exterior, Vivianne looked up, spotting the stained glass. She'd always been intrigued by old churches and their intricate architecture. She'd been raised Catholic but didn't practice it. Still, once a Catholic, always a Catholic.

Sage gave the young couple one last glance. They seemed perfectly content and showed no signs of moving.

"Okay, let's do it. Coming?" Sage asked their companions.

Alec grunted but didn't look up. Maya waved them off. "We'll wait out here for you."

Inside the church was cool and musty. A handful of people knelt at the altar mumbling words of prayer. Lit candles flickered and cast a golden glow over the pews, producing a surreal effect. A tranquil feeling settled over Vivianne. She stared at the awe-inspiring statues that depicted the Stations of the Cross. Above, elaborately painted angels floated on the ceiling. She made her way to the altar with Sage following reverently behind her.

What to do with her life now? She would say a word of prayer. She knelt, bowed her head, and reflected. Her life was a mess and there was no relief in sight. No one would hire a tainted woman. She had no other talents to speak of; she couldn't even make handbags like another fallen woman had.

Sage stayed at her side, awkwardly staring straight ahead. After a few minutes she rose and he followed her out. There was no sign of Alec and Maya outside. The two seemed to have disappeared.

"I wonder where they could have gone?" Sage said, his eyes scanning the immediate area. Before she could answer, he left her behind, rushed down the steps, and began circling the square. Vivianne craned her neck, looking for the couple. The same eerie premonition surfaced. Was she being stalked? A tightness invaded her chest. It became uncomfortable to breathe.

Goose bumps covered her arms. She sensed someone come up behind her, smelled a strong garlicky scent, and turned. A disembodied hand reached out and shoved her. There was nothing she could do to steady herself or regain her footing. Vivianne went flying through the air.

She was conscious of people screaming, of her limbs flailing helplessly, of falling and falling fast, the pavement reaching up to greet her. She tried shielding her face moments before she hit concrete. A jarring pain in her arm forced a cry out of her.

"Call an ambulance," a voice screamed.

Foreign words came at her. She was barely conscious of people surrounding her. Every breath became an effort and her entire arm throbbed. Noises filtered in and out, questions from concerned tourists that she couldn't grasp and wouldn't even attempt to answer.

"Are you all right?"

"Oh, my God, someone call an ambulance."

There were queries in stringent Italian. She should try to sit up, but even the thought of moving nauseated her. Her head felt as if it would burst, and stars exploded before her eyes.

A cool palm reached for her pulse. She was conscious of a man taking charge and of him demanding, "Vicki, talk to me, say something."

Sage. Relief came in the form of his arm around her shoulders. She was incapable of formulating the first word. Sage would take care of her. With a supreme effort Vivianne opened her eyes and stared into an azure sky: blue, calm, and filled with stars. The arm throbbed mercilessly.

"Vicki," Sage persisted, "I want you to concentrate really hard. I'm going to hold up my fingers and I'll need you to tell me how many fingers you see."

Vivianne squinted at Sage. She thought he might be holding up three fingers but the words still wouldn't come. The pain persisted, and she could barely make out his form, much less follow instructions. Feet thudded, and the crowd scattered. The commotion forced her into a seated position. She fell back, and had it not been for Sage's strong arms, would have passed out.

Men yelled in Italian and there was something placed over her nose and mouth. Fingers gently probed her limbs. She flinched where it ached as the world slowly came into focus.

Two hefty men hovered over her. *Medics,* she registered.

"Signora . . ."

"English," Sage said sharply.

"Miss," one of them said in halting English, "you are cut

badly and might have a sprain. We will put you on a stretcher and take you to the hospital."

"No hospital," Vivianne said groggily.

"Eet ees where you need to be. Your bruises should be tended."

She didn't want to go to a hospital. Didn't want to answer prying questions and be forced to give her name. She would be required to fill out paperwork, and then the whole truth would come out. Vivianne's teeth began to chatter. Reality ebbed and flowed. Anxious faces peered down at her. She would be all right. She had to be.

"Help me to my feet," she ordered Sage.

"No way. I'm finding you a doctor." He scooped her up in his arms.

Using her clenched fists she pounded on his back. "No. No. We need to find Alec and Maya."

Sage ignored her. "I need someone who speaks English," he demanded, scanning the crowd.

A scholarly-looking type stepped forward. "I do, sir, quite well. How can I help you?"

"Tell me where I can find the nearest doctor."

The man pointed down a narrow alleyway and reeled off an address. Another onlooker handed Sage Vivianne's sunglasses. She shoved them onto the bridge of her nose and laid her head against Sage's chest. His arms around her provided a safe haven. She buried her nose in his manly scent. Sage thanked the paramedics before heading off. They rolled their eyes, indicating he was crazy.

"Take me back to the hotel," Vivianne demanded when they were halfway down the alley.

"Not in this lifetime. You're hurt and need medical attention."

She sighed. It was useless protesting. Besides, it felt good having him take charge, having him care for her.

Still carrying Vivianne, Sage found the building where

the doctor practiced. He climbed four rickety steps. They entered a shabby room where patients in various stages of distress moaned. Sage set her down in one of the chairs. After about fifteen minutes, an attendant, speaking halting English, took down her information. Another hour elapsed before a female doctor appeared.

Dusk had come by the time they exited but the news was at least good. Her arm wasn't broken and she'd been given relief for her aching head.

"I'm getting us a water taxi," Sage said, his lips close to her ear, his warm breath caressing her skin. "After that, my love, I'm putting you to bed."

My love? She didn't dare make more of it than had been intended. "Bed sounds good," Vivianne murmured groggily.

Sage's arm circling her waist remained a steady anchor. She leaned into him, achingly aware of his hard body and the sensuous smell of a musky cologne. She'd never been so cared for, cherished, tended to. All this time she'd been starving for human affection; now she welcomed his touch.

Sage's voice was deceptively low when he whispered, "You'll tell me later what Vivianne Baxter is doing in Venice, alone."

The sound of her real name jolted her. Vivianne forget about her hurt arm and that only moments ago he'd made her feel safe. How could Sage have found out who she was? She remembered how she'd lost her sunglasses, and that poker face of his when he'd helped her fill out the doctor's paperwork. Easy for him to put two and two together.

"You know who I am?" Vivianne croaked, a sinking feeling in the pit of her stomach.

"I've known since yesterday," Sage confirmed. "And I hope you'll trust me enough to tell me the real story."

Vivianne could only hope he would be open-minded. She badly needed a friend.

Five

"Whadda you think?" Alec asked, holding his sketch pad out so that his rendition of the church could be suitably admired.

He and Maya had wandered over to a little square, picked one of the many trattorias, and taken a seat at an outdoor table. Neither was hungry, so they'd ordered bottled water.

Maya oohed and aahed over the rough sketching. Alec took a swig from the bottle and sat back. Maya's approval meant a lot to him but he wasn't about to blow his cool and show any emotion. He'd mastered the art of keeping his reactions in check. You had to, or people would take advantage of you and know exactly which buttons to press. Alec had manipulated the situation so that they'd lost their unwanted chaperones. The plan all along had been to have Maya to himself.

"You did a great job. You captured the church perfectly," Maya said, holding the sketch up and examining it closely. "Oh, Alec, you're good. Really good."

He knew he was good, but no one had ever admired his work so openly or gushed as loudly as Maya had. He wanted to hug her.

"So tell me about yourself," he said. "What do you want to be when you grow up?"

"I'm studying psychology but haven't decided what I want to do."

"How about a therapist?"

She shrugged. "I don't know. I just know I want to help people."

Alec examined the face of a gold watch that looked expensive. Rolex if he were to guess, or a very good imitation of one. Why would someone Maya's age own expensive jewelry, unless she was rich?

"Is that a Rolex?" Alec asked, curious to see what her reaction might be.

Maya shifted uncomfortably. She fiddled with the watch. "It was a gift for graduating from high school."

An expensive gift. A hand plowed through his dreadlocks. What had he gotten himself into? "Do your folks have money or something?" he asked.

"Depends on what you consider money."

She was being evasive. Maya was different from the other black girls he knew. Her clothing looked like they cost a fortune, and she didn't know street slang. He'd had to translate the most common urban vernacular.

"Money to me means owning your own home, having two vehicles parked in the driveway, cash in the bank."

"My folks work hard for their money," she responded, a bit defensively. "I'm an only child and my parents take good care of me."

Just his luck to get hooked up with a spoiled rich girl. But he liked her. Her innocence in a jaded world was refreshing. Most of the young girls he knew had a hard edge to them. They were interested in what a man could do for them, buy them. But Maya seemed fascinated by simple things he took for granted. She'd been bug-eyed at the nightclub, and was enjoying sitting outdoors, sipping her water and people-watching.

"What about you?" she asked. "What do you want to be when you grow up?"

"An artist," he said, not missing a beat. "Business is a second major."

Maya screwed up her face, thinking. "Artists struggle until they make it big. Some never do."

She sounded like his mother, who was actually supportive but worried that he would end up like her, barely making a living.

"I chose art because I'm good at it; the business major will help put food on the table and a roof over my head. I don't want to answer to the man for the rest of my life. I'd like control of my own destiny."

Maya reflected for a moment. "Good point. Let's go back and look for Sage and Vicki."

Alec made a face. The hell he would, not when he was just getting to know her.

He shook his head. "It's not like we invited them to come along. They invited themselves, I'm sure they can manage on their own."

"That may be so, but they left us sitting on the steps of that church and we just walked away."

Alec took a last swig of water. "They'll get over it. We can apologize later. Sage is probably busy making time with that woman. Bet you anything he'd like to get next to her."

"You said he wanted to get next to me," Maya pointed out.

"My man's hedging his bets. There's something about him that doesn't sit right with me."

"I think he's cute. Besides, he's really nice."

"Cute is as cute does, my mother often says. Something's strange about him traveling alone."

"So are we, for that matter."

"We're students. We took advantage of the student fare."

He was feeling her out, waiting to see how she would answer. When she didn't right away, he probed some more.

"Isn't that why you decided to join this group, because it was relatively cheap?"

"My parents paid for the trip," Maya admitted reluctantly. "I guess they took advantage of the student discount."

"Well, at least your parents could afford to pay. My mother's a housekeeper. She can barely make ends meet. I worked construction every chance I got and barely scraped up the dough."

"What about your father?" Maya asked. "Couldn't he help?"

Boy, she was naive. "I don't have a father," he admitted. *At least not one that I know of.*

"Everyone has a father," Maya said, eyeing him curiously.

"I never met him, so as far as I'm concerned he doesn't exist. He abandoned my mother when she was pregnant." Alec plopped several lira down on the table and stood. Subject closed.

"I think we should find Vicki and Sage," Maya insisted.

"I think we shouldn't." He took her hand. "Come on, Maya, didn't you say you wanted to explore?"

She hesitated. "It's rude to just walk away and leave them."

"Like I said, they'll get over it."

The temperature had risen and Maya took off her cardigan. She wore a tank top underneath and her golden shoulders were exposed. She was beautiful, unaffected by her looks, and vulnerable in a manner that appealed to him. They wandered for a while, paying little attention to a siren in the background.

"Look," Maya, said, spotting an outdoor market. "I love flea markets. Let's see if there are any bargains to be found."

Locals had set up tables and were peddling a variety of wares, everything from tarnished silver to produce. Alec consulted the map, announcing that they were in the district of Cannaregio, otherwise known as the ghetto. They trudged their way down several crowded aisles, stopping when an item caught their interest. Maya bought a pair of cameo earrings and Alec purchased a painting that he could ill afford.

The watercolor was not particularly expensive, but he was on a tight budget and buying the painting meant that he would have to skip some meals not covered in the price of the tour ticket. Oh, well, so be it. He'd been drawn to the art with its picture of houses high on stilts. It was so Venice.

Afterward, they hopped a vaporetto and strolled along the banks of the Grand Canal, finally plopping onto a wooden bench. Speedboats and party boats glided by with people hanging over the railings, waving at them. Alec felt a huge urge to capture it all on paper, but the girl seated next to him was much too distracting. She smelled like freshly squeezed lemons and he wondered what perfume she was wearing. There was something about Maya's wild hair that made him want to run his fingers through it. Her skin was the color of toast and her complexion flawless. He was clearly out of his league, but she was worth exploring.

Alec gave in to the urge to touch her. He ran a finger along her jawline, and her midnight-colored eyes lit up. "Enjoying yourself?" he asked.

"Immensely. You have no idea what it's like to just sit here and not be anyone but myself."

"Why would you have to be anything other than yourself?" Alec asked, the back of his hand grazing her cheek lightly.

"It's expected of me," she said wistfully. "My parents are big on appearances and they tend to be overprotective."

"I'd like to protect you," he said, leaning over to cup her chin and kiss her. Maya surprised him by deepening the kiss. He captured her tongue and began working it. She tasted slightly of this morning's cappuccino, and there was that lemon scent again.

"That was nice," she said when they separated.

Alec realized that she was somewhat of a novice. She might look like a guy magnet but didn't have much experience. He liked that.

"What do your parents do?" he asked.

She hesitated for a moment before answering, "They're businesspeople."

Businesspeople could mean anything. "What kind of business are they in?"

"A little bit of this and a little bit of that."

Another vague answer. She'd confirmed she wasn't some girl from off the street. The pocketbook she carried was expensive, a designer's he didn't recognize. The jeans she wore weren't off the rack. Not the way they fitted, as if they were custom-made.

"I guess we should head back," Alec said reluctantly.

"I'd like to try to make the concert," Maya said.

"Not a bad idea. They're serving a box lunch on the grounds of the Villa San Martini. If we can catch up with Sage and Vicki, we might get there on time."

Holding hands, they slowly retraced their steps.

Vicki and Sage were nowhere in sight when they climbed the church steps. Alec checked out the interior. A handful of people wandered aimlessly, awed by the spectacular architecture, but there was no sign of the couple.

"Looks like they left."

"Can you blame them?"

Maya seemed ticked. "I guess we better consult the map and figure out how to get to this concert," Alec said, coming up beside her.

"I guess so," Maya said, slowly unfolding the map and handing it over. "Here, you look."

Alec was left with the funny feeling inside that he'd displeased her.

Sage had forced Vivianne to take two aspirins and chase them with water. At his insistence she now lay in bed with the blinds drawn, mesmerized by the motion of an overhead fan. He'd called down for room service and they chatted while waiting for their pasta and salads to arrive.

"Where could those two lovebirds have gone?" Vivianne said, stalling the inevitable questions. "They just up and left us."

"More like they wandered off."

Sage chastised himself for not keeping a better eye on Maya. He never should have let her out of his sight, but if he hadn't been around when Vivianne had fallen, who knew where she would have ended up? She needed protection and he was the man.

"I guess they'll show up sometime."

"Tell me about Vivianne Baxter," he said, as Vivianne stared at him wide-eyed. Unable to stop himself, he crossed over to plump up her pillows and help her into a seated position. "I'm waiting."

"What?"

Vivianne's face, free of makeup, was a perfect oval. She looked as if she wanted to cry. But it was the timbre of her voice that clenched his gut and made him want to hold her. Better to check his feelings and give in to the insatiable curiosity that had once made him good at his craft.

"I want to hear all about Vivianne Baxter and how she ended up making headlines," Sage said firmly.

This time she blinked. "Everything there is to know was covered by the media."

"I'd like to hear your version."

The woman Vivianne had been made out to be didn't resemble the frail woman lying here in bed. She flinched visibly, and not just from physical pain.

"You must know I was the spokesperson for WOW," she said. "I had a pretty high-profile position."

"Yes, that I know. You represented the organization beautifully. In fact I listened to some of your speeches, they were quite impressive."

"Nevertheless, I was vilified, my reputation ruined. I lost my job," she went on.

Intrigued, Sage asked the obvious question. "Tell me how that came to be. You never harassed those men the reporters mentioned?"

"I've never mixed business and pleasure," Vivianne said, wincing again. "I've never even dated a man in my organization."

"What about Harold Huggins? He was an employee of yours—a supervisor, to be exact. He says you kept asking him out on dates, that he would go because he was afraid of losing his job. He claims you made advances, that when he resisted you fired him."

"Harold Huggins is a liar. I inherited Harold when the accounting manager resigned. Rather than replace his position, the organization asked me to take over that department along with my other responsibilities. Harold and I had maybe two business dinners. His work performance fell short of my expectations and after numerous warnings, with no effort on his part to shape up, I was forced to let him go. He tried persuading me to keep him on. He even told me he loved me, and that the two of us should hook up."

"Are you implying that he was a man scorned?"

"I'm implying that he was desperate. The man had a wife and two kids at home. His accusations stemmed from his need to keep his job."

Sage didn't know what to believe. Vivianne's explanation sounded plausible. "What about the other men?"

"You don't believe me, do you?" Vivianne cried. "The other men who came forward were clerks who worked for Harold. All were bent on getting ahead. Harold promised them promotions. Most of the high-level positions at WOW are filled by men. I was one of the rare women who made it to the top."

"All of these men conspired against you?" Sage asked, knowing he sounded dubious.

"Yes, they did. I would walk in on them surfing the Internet when they should have been working. Then several checks from corporations mysteriously disappeared."

"You think they misappropriated the funds."

"Yes, but I couldn't prove it."

"But what grounds would they have to accuse you of sexual harassment?"

"I'm a friendly person by nature. A tap on the arm, a warm embrace when greeting employees has always been my style. I should have known better. Physical contact is not appropriate in the workplace. I guess I learned the hard way."

Sage's eyebrows rose. "I'm still not understanding why these men you supervised decided to go screaming to your superior that you hit on them."

Vivianne sighed. "Do you have any idea what it's like to try to manage people who don't want to be managed by a woman? I experienced passive aggressive behavior at its worst."

He nodded. He did know what it was like to attempt to conduct business in a hostile environment, especially when no one trusted you. But he wasn't about to tell Vivianne that.

"The organization was starting to downsize," she continued. "Government funding was cut back and people feared for their jobs. Then there was the matter of the missing checks. We didn't know these companies had made monetary contributions until they began to gripe that they'd never been recognized. WOW began a full-fledged investigation when they discovered the funds were missing."

"And what was the outcome of that investigation? Why did these men go after you?"

"The misappropriation of funds is still being investigated. My employees disliked working for a woman and having her call the shots. Harold felt he should have my job, and his buddies saw me as an obstacle in their way. I suppose they did what they thought they had to do." Vivianne closed her eyes and sighed. "The organization was my entire life, not to mention my livelihood."

Sage wondered where their food was. Vivianne looked tired, and he should let her rest. But interrogation was second nature to him. Her story intrigued him, and her vulnerability made every protective instinct come out. He wanted to provide a strong pair of shoulders on which she could rest her head. A ridiculous notion. Silly and romantic. Unlike him.

"Okay, so these bozos conspired to get you fired," he said, pulling himself together.

"Yes, they did." Vivianne's eyes were tightly closed. A sharp rap on the door forced them open again. "Food's here."

The waiter wheeled in a table and Sage signed the check. Vivianne attempted to protest but Sage shot her a quelling look. After they ate, the conversation resumed.

"I walked in on Harold and his buddies talking several weeks earlier," Vivianne said. "They were planning how they would divvy up the money they'd gotten. When I asked if they'd won the lotto or something, they said yes."

"Interesting. I'd like to hear more about this later. Meanwhile you need to rest."

He saw Vivianne's eyelids start to droop as he let himself out. The protective side of him wanted to hold her in his arms until she slept. Now wasn't the time for romance, however. He had a job to do, a job that paid bills. Better to go in search of Maya.

Sage shut the door softly, leaving visions of the vulnerable, sweet woman behind.

Six

Whatever had possessed her to attend the masked ball? Curiosity, most likely, and a feeling that she would be missing out on a wonderful memory.

Vivianne's arm still throbbed. She ignored it. She sat at the table inside the palace, sipping wine and chatting with a divorced publicist from Manhattan.

There was no sign of Sage, or for that matter, any couple resembling Maya and Alec. Hidden behind a mask, Vivianne felt perfectly at ease. She could be anyone she wanted to be in her rented costume and powdered wig. With the aid of a salesgirl, she'd been transformed into an eighteenth-century beauty. The girl had told her that that the masks had been the only chance for equality in a society where social barriers existed.

Vivianne decided that tonight she would work it. She would flirt and have a good time. She began by practicing on Francine Quinn, the publicist, and the others around her table. They were an eclectic bunch, some outfitted in outrageous costumes. There was a gondolier, a court jester, a monk, several opera stars, and a plump couple outfitted in seventeenth-century regalia. Vivianne suspected they were the Edwardses, simply because they couldn't keep their mouths shut—their midwestern accents were hard to miss.

"What do you do when you're back in the States?" Francine slurred, staring at Vivianne through the slits of her mask. She took another mouthful of wine and swilled it. Several of the men tossed them interested glances as they walked by, largely because Francine's peasant gown had a plunging neckline and her more than adequate breasts spilled forth. Francine boldly made eye contact with the men through the slits of her mask.

"I write speeches," Vivianne said, repeating the same story she'd told Sage. It wasn't an outrageous lie. She *had* written speeches, though it seemed a long time ago.

"We have a lot in common," Francine said. "Do you write for politicians or for a corporation?"

"A corporation."

Vivianne doubted she had anything in common with Francine. The woman was sophisticated, but brash, and seemed to constantly name-drop.

A quartet had begun to play, and several people converged on the dance floor. The members of the Buena Vista group were not the only people here. Their group leader, Angelica, flitted around making sure everyone was having a good time. One of the men openly admiring Francine's assets asked her to dance, and Vivianne used it as an opportunity to wander off.

She scouted the room, looking to see if Sage was around. He'd called often, to check up on her. She'd felt awkward knowing that he knew who she was. She'd kept their conversations brief, and when he suggested they attend the ball together, she'd declined, stating that she didn't feel well enough. Later she'd changed her mind, caught a water taxi with several other guests and made her way here.

Vivianne brushed by several ladies clad in fashionable nineteenth-century gear; they stood in a corner, laughing and checking out men. A large group had taken over the terrace and she headed outdoors, hoping that the cool night air would soothe the headache that was brewing. It was the first time she'd been outside since she'd been pushed. But she figured that with a crowd, no harm could come to her here.

Vivianne replayed the events. Since arriving in Venice she'd had her pocketbook stolen, received a threatening note, and been pushed down several steps. Someone was after her, but why? Wasn't it enough that she'd been disgraced and now had no job?

A man approached wearing a powdered wig and eighteenth-century Venetian attire. He was tall, well built, and stood out from the crowd. She wondered if he had followed her.

"Hi," he said. "Want to dance?"

An American accent, what a relief. She relaxed and decided to have fun with him. Hidden behind her mask she was safe.

"Sure. Why not?"

He offered her his arm. Vivianne took it. They managed to squeeze onto the crowded dance floor. He twirled her around. She darted glances over her shoulder, looking for Sage, but there was no one looking remotely like him to be found.

A young couple stood on the periphery watching the dancing. They were dressed as Romeo and Juliet, and the couple's dark complexion and the man's dreadlocks were a sure giveaway. Maya and Alex. Vivianne was tempted to race off the dance floor and join them. She hadn't seen them since the day of her fall, though Maya had called to inquire how she was. If Maya was there, Sage must be somewhere around.

Sage. What was it about him that fascinated her? He was mysterious and not entirely open, but the same could be said of her. He'd told her that he was in the securities business, and he seemed to have an abnormal fascination with a woman at least a decade younger. The thought occurred that his interest in Maya might not be romantic, as she'd initially thought. It was really none of her business.

"Hey, you're a million miles away," her dance partner said.

Vivianne missed a step; she recovered beautifully and apologized. The stranger drew her closer. His eyes glittered behind the mask. They continued to dance.

When the music stopped, Vivianne excused herself and went back outside hoping to find Maya and Alec. Several couples had sought the outdoors and she spotted Alec's dreadlocks before he saw her.

Vivianne approached the couple.

"Hi," she said. "Having fun?"

"This is so cool," Maya responded. "I would never have thought in my wildest dreams that I would be here at a masked ball, dancing under a Venetian moon."

"Vicki," Alec greeted, "you look wonderful. Sage mentioned you weren't coming because you weren't feeling well. Are you fully recovered?"

"I'm feeling much better, thank you," she answered.

"Good. We were worried. We owe you an apology for disappearing. We left to have a drink and time got away from us."

Vivianne acknowledged Alec's apology with a nod of her head. She held no animosity toward them. They were young and obviously in the throes of lust.

"Sage is somewhere," Maya said, looking around. "He'll be glad to see you."

Just the sound of his name caused Vivianne's heartbeat to accelerate. She was too old to have feelings like this.

"I'd like to say hi. Is he wearing a costume?"

"Yes, we got him into the spirit of things with a little persuasion. We even convinced him to buy a mask. He makes a very handsome footman." Maya pointed to the other side of the terrace. "He was over there. Go see if you can find him."

Vivianne got the message. They wanted to be alone.

Alec placed an arm around Maya's shoulders and they

wandered off. Vivianne decided to go look for Sage. *Why not?* she thought. She removed her mask and headed off in the direction they'd pointed. As she wove her way through clusters of people she had the peculiar sensation that someone dogged her every move. Vivianne's trepidation grew as she sidestepped several drunken revelers.

When a hand clamped down on her shoulder, she jumped. A man's voice said, "I wondered where you'd disappeared to."

It was her suitor, the man she had danced with.

"I needed some air," Vivianne said. "It was stuffy inside."

He came up alongside her. "Me too. Let's take a walk."

Before she could answer, his grip on her arm tightened, and he tugged her along, propelling her across the terrace and down a steep flight of steps.

In the gardens, Vivianne suppressed the panic that was building. If she made a big fuss it might appear that she was overreacting. The man, although overzealous, hadn't threatened her.

They were halfway across the lawn when a shadow blocked their path. "Is everything okay?" a deep voice asked.

Vivianne recognized the timbre, it was Sage. Her companion, surprised by the sudden intrusion, loosened his grip and Vivianne stumbled. She was never so glad to see anyone in her life.

"Hi. I heard you were here," Sage said. "Who's your friend?"

Prepared to make introductions, Vivianne turned to her companion, but he darted off like a shot, racing across the lawn and into the shadows.

"Must be my deodorant," Sage joked.

"I doubt that. His behavior was strange. He practically dragged me out here."

"You need to be careful," Sage said, taking her hand and heading back across the lawn and toward the palace. "Let's grab a drink and you can tell me all about your encounter."

Nothing to tell, really, except she was scared.

Inside, the party was in full swing. Several guests had had too much to drink and were singing bawdy melodies. Sage got them drinks and they found seats at the back of the ballroom. He did indeed make a handsome footman. All that beautiful brocaded material highlighting his bronze skin.

"Are all your aches and pains gone?" he asked, his eyes scanning the room, looking for someone.

Maya, Vivianne surmised, a streak of jealousy shooting through her. "I feel better than I did when you last saw me," she answered.

She felt calmer now, just sitting there next to him. Her recent encounter had shaken her to the core and she still didn't know what to make of it.

"Will you be going to Murano tomorrow?" Sage inquired.

She'd been looking forward to the trip, melding with a crowd and playing tourist.

"Count on it."

"Good. Then you can help me pick out souvenirs. I've got friends who would be majorly disappointed if I didn't bring them back something."

Friends. Did those friends include a special girl? The thought that there was a woman in his life made her feel unsettled.

"What are you looking to buy?" she asked carefully, and held her breath waiting for him to answer.

"Just some knickknacks, nothing too expensive. My mother collects miniature animals and a friend collects paperweights."

He specialized in vague answers and she still hadn't found out what she needed to.

"I'd be delighted to help," Vivianne responded. "I love to shop."

Sage tossed back his drink, and set the tumbler on the table.

"By chance did you run into Alec and Maya?" he asked, his eyes scanning the room, his body on alert.

"As a matter of fact I did. About fifteen minutes ago, out on the terrace."

Sage was up like a shot. "I need fresh air. Join me."

It was as if he was obsessed with the girl, but they didn't seem to match. Something strange was definitely going on here. Why not ask?

"What's the story with you and Maya?"

His answer was succinct and to the point. "No story. We're friends. Come, let's go."

She resented the way he gave orders. Still, she didn't want to be alone and Sage's company assured her that the man who'd asked her to dance wouldn't return. On reflection, he'd been too eager to get her alone, and his reaction to Sage had been downright peculiar. If he'd hadn't had bad intentions, why would he run?

Outside, Vivianne walked alongside Sage as he searched the crowd for the young couple. The Edwardses, who'd removed their masks, came up to them. Bonnie seemed flushed. She fanned herself while her husband nursed a beer.

"Hey," she said, her midwestern twang even more pronounced, "you haven't been around, Vicki, we missed you."

"I'm back now," Vivianne assured her with a wave of her hand. Sage nodded, and headed down a steep flight of steps and into the gardens. Vivianne said a hasty good-bye and hurried after him.

Alec and Maya had found a secluded spot in a remote part of the garden. They sat under a tree, removed their stifling masks, and listened to the sounds of revelry from a distance. Alec had wanted to get away from the crowd. When he suggested they take a walk Maya had gladly agreed.

Maya, having had enough of Alec's reticence, broke the silence.

"We're leaving for Rome in two days," she said. "There's bound to be awesome architecture that you can sketch."

Alec plucked a handful of grass. His voice sounded dreamy when he replied. "Good as Rome sounds, I'm tempted to stay right here. I like Venice."

"You're thinking of abandoning the tour?"

"Yep." He reached for her hand and raised the palm to his lips. Maya's whole body trembled. Alec made her feel like no guy had before. "Stay in Venice with me. We'll catch up with the tour later."

Tempting as it sounded, she'd never done anything like this. She'd been taught to play by the rules. But spending time alone with Alec would be heaven. There would be no schedule to follow, and she wouldn't have to be nice to people she had little in common with. She'd get to know what he was all about.

"If we do that, how will we get to Rome?" she asked.

"There's the train. I don't have a lot of money but I've heard Euro rail is relatively inexpensive, especially for students."

"I have money," she offered. "Plenty of it."

Alec's tone grew gruff; it was as if she'd insulted him. "I don't need your money, I can manage."

"It's money I saved up. Let me help you."

His golden-eyed glare caused her not to press the point. What was it with him? Why did he seem so upset by her offer? It was only money and she had a lot to share. He didn't have to know who her parents were. Their stature would only intimidate him. He'd told her often enough how he felt about wealthy people. Snobs, he called them, resenting his mother having to work as a housekeeper.

Maya hadn't exactly lied. She'd saved up her allowance so that she wouldn't have to rely on her parents for spending money. She would gladly share her money with him.

Alec leaned over and kissed her. "You're sweet but I can't accept your money."

Maya felt the world spin. She squeezed her eyes shut. The ground tilted up, then down again. Alec pulled her onto his lap; a finger stroked her bodice, outlining one taut nipple. "Maya?"

"Yes, Alec?"

"I want to make love to you."

She gulped. No one had ever been that direct with her. She wanted to make love with him too, but she was inexperienced and he was a man of the world. Would he make fun of her? Guess that sex, pitiful as it had been, had been limited to a couple of fumbling boys? Alec, you could tell, was anything but a fumbler. He'd taken charge of every situation. She was in over her head.

She would fake it. Maya fumbled with the laces on the ostentatious dress until it fell off her shoulders. Alec now had full access to her breasts. She heard his sharp intake of breath and then felt his exploring fingers. She'd never experienced such tingly feelings and decided to simply enjoy.

"Touch me," Alec said, settling her hand over his crotch.

Touch him. Oh, God, what is he expecting me to do? She couldn't make love right here, out in the open. Sex had usually taken place in a tiny dorm room, or an expensive hotel one of her boyfriends had rented, not on the grass. This would be a new experience.

"What's wrong?" Alec asked when she became deadly still. "You change your mind?"

"I don't know about this," she said hesitantly.

"No one's around. They're inside, drinking their brains out and stomping around that pathetic dance floor."

"I know, but . . ."

"Look, if you don't want to, just say no." Alec sounded annoyed.

She wanted so much to please him. He had fascinated her from the moment she laid eyes on him. Maya's fingers tentatively reached out to stroke his crotch. Alec groaned. He peeled the bodice from her shoulders and buried his head between her breasts. His dreads grazed her nipples and her body came alive. He lifted her skirt and stroked her thighs, sliding a thumb under her underpants until he found her pulsing center. He worked the nub until she panted. Maya squirmed against him, wanting more. When he kissed her again, all rational thought left her head. It no longer mattered that they were outdoors.

Every sense heightened, she listened to the music from a distance. A ballad played, soft and romantic. Maya inhaled the smell of freshly mown grass and she stared up at an orange moon. Losing her skirt, she lay flat on her back and let the moonbeams play across her. It was an intoxicating feeling, lying naked here. It made her feel womanly and wanton when Alec settled on top of her.

Crunching footsteps headed their way. With a muttered expletive, Alec jumped up. "Talk about bad timing."

Maya scrambled for her clothing. Alec helped her find her skirt. She put it on quickly and laced up her bodice.

"Maya, Alec," Sage's voice called.

What was it with him? Why wouldn't he leave them alone?

A second set of footsteps indicated someone was with him. Alec swore again, and placed an arm around her.

Two shadows swiftly approached.

"What's with this guy?" Alec hissed. "He's got this obsession with you."

Maya held her breath as Sage and his companion came closer. She made out a female form. Good, he had Vicki with him.

"I've been looking for you," Sage said, peering through the shadows at them. "Why are you out here?"

Maya was glad he couldn't see her heated face and her haphazardly laced-up bodice.

"We decided to take a walk," she jabbered. "I needed fresh air and Alec was nice enough to accompany me."

"I bet," Sage responded skeptically.

There he was, acting like her father again, as if he owned her. The thought occurred that Alec might be right: Sage's interest in her wasn't purely platonic. He kept popping up in the most unexpected places, as if he were shadowing her. Instead of feeling flattered, she just felt annoyed. Vicki was closer to his age and more his style.

"We were thinking of leaving," Sage said. "Are you ready to call it a night?"

"We aren't," Alec answered rudely. "We planned on exploring the grounds. Alone."

"You've got to be up at the crack of dawn if you plan on taking the tour tomorrow," Sage cautioned. "A good night's sleep won't hurt."

"I said we weren't ready," Alec growled.

"What about you, Maya? Didn't you say you were looking forward to seeing Murano? The museum is one of the highlights of this trip."

"And I am looking forward to seeing Murano. Good night, Sage."

Maya was furious and resented being treated like a child. She was twenty, too old to be told what to do, and by a virtual stranger. Sage's attention, initially flattering, now cramped her style. It was Alec she was interested in.

"Come on, Sage," Vivianne said, asserting herself. "I'm tired. Let's find a water taxi to take us home." Grabbing Sage's arm, she hurried him off.

"Don't stay out too late," Sage admonished over his shoulder. "There are some unsavory characters about."

Maya hadn't a clue what he was talking about, nor did she care. All she knew was that she wanted to be with Alec.

Seven

"Have you seen Maya and Alec?" Sage asked, approaching the table where Vivianne and the Edwardses were chatting on their last night in Venice.

"Can't say that I have."

Sage actually looked distraught, and she wondered what the two had been up to, to bring that about.

Vivianne was dressed from head to toe in what had become her signature black. She adjusted tinted glasses and squinted at Sage. The Edwardses, oblivious, grinned up at him. They'd spotted Vivianne as she walked by the cocktail lounge, and invited her to join them for a drink. She hadn't wanted to be rude so she'd sat down and ordered a spritzer. One drink had led to another, and it had been difficult to get away. Sage was just the excuse she needed.

"Please sit down," the Edwardses said, gesturing to the vacant chair.

"Maybe later. I'm looking for those kids." He scanned the room with a worried expression. Vivianne had never seen him so out of sorts.

"Alec and Maya have been missing for hours," he mumbled.

"They were at breakfast this morning," Bonnie Edwards offered. "That Maya is one cute girl."

"Have you checked with the front desk?" Vivianne asked, "Maya might have left you a message."

"Good thought," Sage said, bounding off. He turned back. "Come with me."

Sage had provided just the opening she needed. Vivianne excused herself and followed him to the lobby, glad to escape. The Edwardses, nice as they were, had chatted on incessantly, talking about their farm and their two grown kids who'd been left to run it. She had little in common with them.

Sage approached the desk clerk, who was busy with other people. When it was their turn, the handsome middle-aged clerk smiled over half-moon glasses. "May I help you?"

Sage seemed at a loss for words. When he didn't answer, Vivianne nudged him. "You wanted to ask a question?"

"Please check and see if Maya Gabriel has left me a message," he said.

"Your name, sir?"

"Sage Medino."

"Are you staying here?"

Sage provided his room number. The clerk checked a cubby hole behind him and returned empty-handed.

"I'm sorry, sir, she did not."

"Do you have a phone I can use?"

"I can call her room if you would like."

"Do that."

The clerk punched buttons on his computer and frowned. "Ms. Gabriel has checked out, sir."

"What?"

Sage looked as if he were close to having a heart attack and Vivianne was forced to take over. "Try Alec Randolf's room," she said.

The clerk pushed more buttons, this time making a tssking sound. "Looks like Mr. Randolf has also checked out."

Sage's crude expletive made the desk clerk frown. Vivianne took his arm and hurried him off. "Come on, you look like you could use a drink. We'll take a walk and figure out something."

Outside, peachy hues coated the pastel-colored buildings and a Technicolor sunset filled the sky. Vivianne walked besides a grim-faced Sage, who looked as if he had lost his best friend. They crossed a bridge and entered a tiny square where a few old men played bocci.

She spotted a vine-covered restaurant that was at least three stories high with tables and chairs out front.

"Let's order some wine and talk," Vivianne said, practically tugging Sage into the pretty little courtyard.

"I need to find Maya," Sage muttered. "I can't afford to have her disappear."

"Why is keeping tabs on Maya so important to you?" she asked.

Sage looked visibly shaken by the question. Before he could answer, a rotund woman wearing a long white apron bore down on them.

"Signor, signora. Come in," she greeted. "You are American, yes?"

"Yes, we're American," Vivianne responded. "Come on, Sage, one quick drink won't hurt."

Sage, still looking as if he would rather be anywhere but here, followed the portly woman's lead. She seated them at a battered table. A trellis of climbing vines formed a picturesque backdrop, and the fragrant smell of roses filled the air. Muted conversation came from the surrounding tables.

Two carafes of wine were set down before them, along with a basket of freshly baked rolls.

"Will that be all, signor?" the woman asked.

"That will be all for now," Vivianne answered since Sage still seemed preoccupied.

Vivianne poured the red wine and handed Sage his glass. "Now," she said, "suppose you tell me why you've been shadowing that little girl and why it's so important you not lose her?"

"What makes you think I'm shadowing Maya?" Sage asked, staring into his glass of wine but not drinking it.

"Because you've hardly left her side. You've made a point of remaining close to her even when she and Alec clearly want to be alone. You've become an unwelcome third wheel."

She actually got a smile out of him. His heavy mood seemed to have lifted. "Oh, come on, I wasn't that bad," he joked.

"Oh, come on, you were. At first I thought you were interested in her, but now I'm not sure."

Sage threw his head back and roared. "Interested in Maya? She's a child. I'm almost twice her age. I like my women more seasoned."

"Maya's twenty years old. She told me so herself."

"And I'm thirty-seven. As adorable as Maya is, she and I have little in common. I like women who have lived a life."

"Well, that's a new one. Most men your age are looking for arm candy, youthful women, pleasing to the eye."

"I find women in their thirties and forties more my style. You, for example, have Maya beat, hands down."

Vivianne blushed. Was he coming on to her or simply being gracious? She decided it must be the latter. She hadn't done a thing to make herself attractive, not once this trip. Her only indulgence had been keeping her toenails painted a ridiculous hot pink.

"So, what's the story?" Vivianne said. "What is it with you and Maya?"

Sage gulped his wine and seemed to debate. Vivianne sipped her drink and waited for him to speak.

"Maya's a job," he said.

"Job?" What did that mean? Sage made it sound like he was on some undercover assignment. She thought about all the peculiar things that had happened to her since getting to

Venice. What if . . . what if Sage was in some way involved? What if he was an unsavory character? Nonsense. He'd always been there when she needed him. He'd come to her rescue more often than she cared to think. But what if it was all by design?

Vivianne decided to keep things light. "This all sounds very hush-hush. What is it that you really do? Are you on an undercover assignment?"

Sage grinned at her. "You can call it that. I'm an ex-FBI agent and Maya's a side job."

He wasn't a criminal, thank God. "Why does that sweet child need protecting?" Vivianne asked. "And how come you're retired? You're awfully young."

"I'm not retired. I was forced out of my job. It's a long story and a boring one."

"I have no place to go and I'm willing to listen. How does Maya fit into the picture?"

Sage's long fingers circled the bowl of his glass. "Maya's parents hired me to make sure she stays out of trouble."

"They must be important. Average people don't hire a bodyguard to look out for their daughter."

Bees droned around them, almost drowning out her words. Orange and black butterflies fluttered overhead, landing occasionally on flowers spilling from huge clay pots. Vivianne drummed her fingers against the table's wooden surface, trying her best to put all the pieces together. Maya Gabriel? Was that name supposed to ring a bell?

"Maya Gabriel," she said out loud. "If she was a sports personality I would know. I don't think she's an R and B singer. Could be she's the child of an ambassador, or a high-profile government type?"

Sage stared straight ahead giving nothing away. She stared at his gorgeous face, thinking he looked more like a male model than a law enforcement officer.

"That's it. That's it!" she cried excitedly. "Maya's parents are famous and you've been hired to protect her. Stan and Nona Gabriel are one of Hollywood's most beautiful couples. They've got to be in their forties, the right age to have Maya as a daughter. Is that who she is, Sage? Stan and Nona's daughter? She must be worth a small fortune."

Sage drained the last drop of liquid from his glass and poured himself another. "I signed a confidentiality statement with my client. I can't confirm or deny your comment."

She guessed she'd hit pay dirt. The Italian paparazzi would go crazy if they found out. Unbeknownst to Buena Vista Tours they'd signed on two newsworthy people, one famous and the other infamous.

Vivianne sipped her wine and strategized how to go about pumping Sage for more information. She couldn't imagine why an ex-FBI agent would be reduced to following a young girl around. There was more here than met the eye.

"You said you were forced to give up your career?" she asked, skeptically. "Why is that?"

Sage told her about the cocaine bust and the case he'd been working on. The guy had been a prominent millionaire, well respected and viewed by the world as a philanthropist. Sage and his partner had wangled their way into his graces. They'd been at a party when a speedboat filled with cocaine pulled up at the man's waterfront home and unloaded its cargo. They'd made the arrest, and the cocaine they'd confiscated had later disappeared. Sage had been the last person in the evidence room and the finger had pointed to him. He'd been suspended pending investigation and later forced to resign.

"Why were you singled out?" Vivianne asked, suspecting there were large gaps in his story. It sounded somewhat farfetched, but so did her story, for that matter. "Weren't there other agents assigned to the case?"

"The FBI is a very political organization. I was up for a

directorship, a coveted position. Rarely has an African American been considered."

"You're saying bigotry had something to do with it?"

"I'm saying it played a part. The United States isn't as open-minded a place as we'd like to believe. There was a lot of pressure put on me to resign."

Could someone have set him up? Vivianne had suspected her own issues resulted from being a black woman in a prominent position. Most of the male board members at WOW were white. Harold Huggins, the man who took her job, was white, and so were most of his subordinates. Even the majority of welfare recipients were white, contrary to popular belief, but at least these people had come forward to support her.

How awful for Sage if what he was saying was true. He'd told her he'd been with the FBI for ten years and he obviously loved his job. She was sure he'd been good at it.

"You resigned without a fight," Vivianne said, regarding him carefully.

"I fought like hell to clear my name," Sage answered, cracking his knuckles loudly. The rivets around his mouth deepened as he went on. "After a while you get worn down. I had to think of what was best for my family and how a scandal would impact them."

There was a sinking feeling in the pit of Vivianne's stomach when she asked, "Family? Are you married?"

"I'm divorced."

She exhaled the breath she didn't realize she was holding. She didn't want to be attracted to a married man. "You mentioned family."

"My parents and grandparents, my brothers and sisters. I couldn't afford to have them featured in the papers so I decided to cut my losses and leave before that could happen."

"You took the easy way out."

Sage glared at her, his jaw still working. "I took the prudent way out. There are times you just can't fight city hall."

She was in no position to be judgmental. Her situation hadn't been that different, and despite her denials of wrongdoing she'd still lost her job. In retrospect, she should never have invited male subordinates out to dinner, regardless of whether there'd been legitimate business to discuss. Her caring personality had been what had gotten her into the mess. Innocent hugs and words of reassurance had been portrayed as her hitting on men.

Their hostess interrupted. "How about trying my pasta?" she asked, drying her hands on an oversize apron.

Sage looked to Vivianne but she was busy with the menu. "Give us another minute."

"Let me know when you're ready," the woman said, walking away.

"Believe me, I tried everything to prove my innocence," Sage said when the woman was out of earshot.

Vivianne shut the menu. "But who would have set you up?"

"Anyone interested in the directorship."

Against her better judgment, she grabbed Sage's hand. "You've got to fight and get your job back."

"I've been thinking about that," he admitted. "Time away has helped put things into perspective. I've thought about contacting my boss when I get back. He's always been supportive. Right now, though, I need to keep the only job I have. I have to find Maya."

"I'll help you," Vivianne said, tossing some lira on the table. "What happens if you aren't able to track Alec and Maya down?"

Sage looked as if the thought was incomprehensible. "Then I'll stay in Venice until I do."

"And I'll stay with you," she said impulsively.

He seemed surprised. Shocked. Truth was, she was tired

of playing tourist. She was sick of being herded back and forth. She'd had it with pretending that falling from grace didn't matter. She missed her job and missed helping people. And she liked Sage Medino more than she was willing to admit.

How this would all end was anyone's guess.

Eight

"I'm paying you guys good money to get the job done," a muffled voice growled through the earpiece.

Guido held the phone away from his ear, rolling his eyes as the American babbled on. Guido's English wasn't that good but he got the message. The American who'd hired him was angry. So excitable these people were. Things didn't happen overnight.

He'd agreed to the job because he needed the money and the American had plenty of it. It wasn't Guido's fault that every time he'd come close to scaring the *bella negra* her boyfriend showed up. Guido was a small-time crook, hired through a friend of a friend to scare the black American woman. He wasn't paid to ask questions, just to get the job done. And the American had given him a hefty advance.

He listened as the man rambled on and Guido motioned to his buddies to keep the noise down. Covering the mouthpiece, he hissed in rapid Italian, "Boss says you guys screwed up, he wants the job done."

His friends, unconcerned, continued to swill beer. They were more focused on getting drunk than making the American happy. It would be his neck on the line if he didn't do something about the woman.

The muffled voice on the other end continued. "Vivianne Baxter needs to be silenced once and for all. Got it? She knows too much."

Guido didn't know what the woman knew, nor did he care. He just knew that if he didn't finish the job he wouldn't get paid.

"Sí, signor, capisco," he said. "We'll get to it."

"Damn right, you will," the American yelled. "Next time, have someone who knows what they're doing finish the job."

"Aye. Aye."

Last time, they'd come so close to teaching the woman a lesson. Until the boyfriend had showed up. The American he'd subcontracted with, coward that he was, had run for his life. The man, an expatriate, had come well recommended. He'd assured Guido it would be easy to get the black woman away from the group. There'd been no plans to hurt her, just bang her up a bit. Unfortunately, the man built like a *bagno* had appeared, and the American ran, pocketing the hefty advance Guido had paid him. He hadn't seen him since.

"Got it?" the American screamed. "I'm not paying you guys another lira until you scare the living hell out of Vivianne Baxter once and for all."

"I hear you, boss," Guido said.

He heard him loud and clear. The whole place heard him. Guido knew enough English to know that the man was serious. Business was slow and he needed every lira. Guido needed to let his buddies know it was time to get busy.

"Hear this," the American yelled. "Vivianne Baxter is staying on in Venice. My sources confirmed that she is. You guys have a few days to send her a message. If nothing happens, I'm replacing you."

"Give me a couple of days and everything will be taken care of," Guido quickly assured him.

"You got two days," the man said before slamming down the phone.

Guido approached his friends warily. "We take care of business today," he said firmly.

The men grumbled and downed another mouthful of beer.

"Oggi?"

"Today?"

"Yes, today."

They set down their bottles and the big guy called Tony rounded them up.

"Let's go," Guido said, leading them out.

The job would be completed. They all needed the money.

Alec ran his hand across Maya's smooth skin. He inhaled the intoxicating scent of her perfume, mingling with the pungent aroma of sex. Maya's hair fanned across his chest, tickling his nipples. She sighed and nestled comfortably against him. Alec's hands cupped her bare buttocks and pressed her firmly up against him. Maya kissed his neck. He slipped on a condom and eased himself inside her and began a slow thrust. Maya groaned.

The room that they'd checked into was airy, large, and spotless. Huge fans whirred from the ceiling and the curtains at the open window fluttered in the breeze. Outside, Italian peddlers hawked their wares and the sounds of tourists' chattering drifted in. The water taxi driver had brought them to the inexpensive pensione the hotel clerk recommended. As an added bonus, breakfast was included in the price.

As he continued his exploration of her body, Maya's contented purrs filled the room. Her inexperience showed and he liked that. It was refreshing to be with a woman who didn't know the ropes. He was in total control, and control was important to Alec. That way, his emotional buttons didn't get pushed. Giving your heart to someone left you open to hurt. And Alec had no intention of ever getting hurt.

That was another reason he'd always chosen his girlfriends carefully. They were usually women that he would never get emotionally attached to. Women who couldn't interfere with his master plan. His focus was on graduating from school.

After that, his business degree would help put food on the table and a roof over his head. But his real love was art. Until that dream was realized, he had no time for a steady girlfriend or a relationship that required his emotional presence.

Maya's contented sighs got his attention. Alec continued to thrust, filling Maya up fully. She arched like a cat, trapping him inside her. He quickly adjusted his rhythm. They'd bonded from the moment they'd met, but anything beyond friendship was impossible, not when they came from such different worlds.

Maya, Alec guessed, came from a life of privilege, a life he knew nothing about. Her clothing, though simple, was expensive. She spoke standard American English and not urban vernacular. Street slang was lost on her.

Alec eased onto his back. Maya looked down on him. Her beautiful face was flushed with emotion, her copper skin held tinges of pink. Maya's perfectly formed breasts jutted forward, the nipples just begging to be captured. He suckled on one until it pebbled. Maya sighed and threw back her head.

Alec felt a rush of exhilaration. No one knew where they were. It was just him and her. They were free of the constant intrusions. Free of Sage. She was staying with him of her own free will. They could make love until the wee hours of the morning if that's what they chose.

Alec lay back, eased on another condom and let Maya ride him. He gave another playful thrust. Maya squealed, her expression changing when he increased his efforts. Blood surged in his head. He refused to think, and for the first time in a long while gave in to his feelings. Giving a final thrust, he let go. Maya's breathing matched his own. She bucked against him, and he exploded, hurling them into a place where feelings were raw. What Alec had approached as fun had turned into something much more. He needed to be careful.

* * *

The remaining people from the Buena Vista tour group were preparing to leave. They trickled onto the water taxi, clutching souvenirs and saying good-bye. The last to board were Kiana Lewis and the Edwardses.

Sage and Vivianne stood on the dock waving. Angelica, their guide, was the last to get on.

"Please call the Buena Vista office if you need anything," she said, finding a seat. "Make sure you have the number."

Sage patted the breast pocket of his shirt. "Got it right here."

Kiana Lewis hung over the edge of the boat tossing out an invitation. "I'll be waiting for you in Rome," she yelled, deliberately ignoring Vivianne.

Sage's eyes avoided her partially exposed breasts. Thank God the taxi started up and he was saved from answering.

"What's the plan?" Vivianne asked as the boat headed out to the Grand Canal.

"We go back to the Metropole and ask around. Someone had to see Alec and Maya leave."

"Okay. We'll start there."

They'd decided to remain at the same hotel in the event that Maya and Alec showed up. The lobby seemed busier than usual when they entered. A long line waited at the reception desk and several tourists examined maps, chattering away in a smattering of languages. A female clerk at the desk patiently answered even the most ridiculous question.

"Buon giorno," she greeted them when they approached.

"Buon giorno. Comé sta?"

The receptionist beamed at them, pleased that Sage had made the effort to speak to her in Italian.

"I'm quite well, thank you. How may I help you?"

"We're trying to locate our friends," Vivianne said, speaking up. "The young man has dreadlocks and the girl has wild hair. They're about my complexion." She stroked her forearm, to emphasize her point.

"Ah, yes, I know who you are speaking of. They are, what you call, good-looking."

"Exactly."

"They are in love with Venice. They are in love with each other," the woman chattered.

"Yes, I suppose," Sage answered, cutting her off. He needed information and quickly. No time for irrelevant small talk.

Maya had been out of his sight for almost two days. She and Alec could be anywhere now. He had no idea what he would tell the Gabriels when they called his international cell phone. But the time difference bought him at least a few precious hours.

"The man with the crazy hair and his girlfriend checked out a while back," the clerk said, repeating what they already knew.

"What's a while back?" Sage demanded.

"A couple of days ago."

"Do you know where they were heading?"

The clerk shrugged expansively and sighed. "They asked if I knew of places that were less expensive than this. I mentioned there were several, if you were willing to share a bath. The girl didn't like that. She thought sharing a bath was strange."

"Did you give them the names of any hotels?" Sage asked.

"I told them about the Hespario, which is a good value for the money. It is quiet and overlooks the Canale di Cannaregio. It is also walking distance to the train station. They said they might want to go to the countryside. I mentioned the Bernardi Semenzato, which is probably the best value of them all. The main hotel is affordable but the annex is even cheaper."

"And where is that located?" Sage interrogated.

"Right off the Strada Nuova and near the Rialto."

"Thank you. You have been most helpful," Sage said, taking Vivianne's hand. "Let's go. Do you have your map with you?"

"In my purse."

He released her hand so she could find the map, and then took it again. Vivianne's heart thumped, though she was determined to maintain her composure. Sage's presence wreaked havoc with her emotions. You'd have to be immune not to be attracted to him. Having him close almost made her forget about the strange things that had happened to her in Venice. But it was hard to dismiss a threatening note.

Outside, a cool breeze rippled off the canal and several tourists were seated on the sidewalks having an early lunch.

"Are we walking or taking a boat?" Vivianne asked, using her free hand to consult the map.

Despite his worried expression, Sage managed a smile. "What do you feel like?"

"A vaporetto. We can cruise down the canal and gaze at all those wonderful pastel-colored houses. It will help get your mind off of Maya."

"Good idea. We'll head for the Hespario first."

"Capital plan."

Ten minutes later they were on board a speedboat heading for the Cannale di Cannaregio and the Hespario. A smaller craft followed at a distance. Vivianne paid little attention to the boat and the four men seated aboard, though one of them was hard to miss, outfitted in red.

She placed a comforting arm around Sage's shoulders and hoped her voice sounded more confident than she felt. "Don't worry. We'll find Alec and Maya. African Americans in Venice stand out like a sore thumb."

"I have to find Maya," Sage repeated, more to himself than to her.

"We'll find her."

The boat behind them picked up speed and came dangerously close to the back of the vaporetto. The man seated across from Vivianne swore softly in Italian. The woman next to him crossed herself, and scowled at the approaching craft. They muttered curses in Italian that Vivianne didn't understand.

"Mama mia," grumbled a young man carrying a loaf of bread and a bag with bottles of red wine. *"Attenzione."*

The taxi picked up speed, leaving a large wake behind it. The speedboat accelerated, closing in on them. Vivianne could see the men more clearly now. They had olive complexions and wore sunglasses, even the man in red. Two of them swilled beer.

"Those jerks are trying to get us killed," Sage said as their taxi pulled into the dock to let the boat by. There was a huge crash and the water taxi came close to capsizing. The people aboard screamed as they went flying.

"Let's get off," Sage said, helping Vivianne up after he had righted himself. "Those bozos obviously have had too much to drink."

Vivianne followed the stream of people surging off. Periodically, she looked over her shoulder to see if Sage was behind her, but in the crush of humanity they became separated.

She had one foot on the dock when a hand clamped down on her wrist. She swayed precariously and the grip tightened. At first she thought it was someone trying to help her, but as the pressure on her wrist increased, she was convinced this was no helping hand. The arm that had been hurt was close to being ripped from its socket.

"Ouch," Vivianne said. "Let go. You're hurting me." A mean-looking face shielded by wraparound sunglasses glared at her. "I can manage on my own."

The man showed no signs of loosening his hold. Two

muscle-bound goons stood behind him, grinning. Where was Sage when she needed him?

Others trying to get off grew impatient; they pushed and shoved, muttering rudely. Vivianne wanted to scream but feared she would be labeled a hysterical American. Could she be overreacting? Who in their right mind would try kidnapping a woman surrounded by people?

"Come on, *bella,*" the man with the grip on her arm urged. "Allow me to help you off."

The passengers behind her had had enough. They scrambled past.

"Scusi," they said, sliding by.

"Scusi."

Vivianne had no choice but to get off with them. The minute she set foot on the dock, the two thugs came alongside her. Each took one arm, and the man who initially grabbed her brought up the rear. A blunt object jabbed into her back. It was worse than she had imagined. She was being held at gunpoint and was being tugged in the direction of the speedboat, where one man remained behind the wheel.

Screaming was not an option now, not with a gun poking into her back. Still no sign of Sage. Suddenly the man to her right grunted and loosened his grip. Doubling over, he fell to his knees. Blood poured from the back of his head. The others, momentarily distracted, stared at him.

"Run, Vivianne run," Sage called from someplace close by. He held the remnants of a broken wine bottle in his hand. She surmised he'd gotten the bottle from the boy with the package. A shot whizzed by her ear and the scene turned into pure bedlam as people ran for their lives. More shots followed and the passengers dove for cover.

Somehow Vivianne made her legs work. Adrenaline pumped through her as she picked up speed. She glanced over her shoulder, and saw Sage wrestling with the man with the gun. The gun fell from the man's hand and Sage kicked it into the water. The others, who had provided backup, abandoned their friend and tugged the wounded man along.

Two policmen appeared, weapons drawn.

"Alt," they shouted in unison.

The men ignored them. Sage wrestled the gunman to the ground and began punching him.

One of the policemen fired at the escaping men but they jumped into the waiting speedboat and roared off.

"Alt," the policemen called again, this time pointing their guns at Sage and the man who'd tried to abduct her.

Still shaken up, Vivianne cried, "No. No, you're after the wrong man. He tried to help me. That man in red was abducting me."

The policemen began screaming at her in rapid Italian.

Vivianne searched for words to make them understand. *"Non parlo Italiano."* It was the only sentence she'd retained from the guide book.

"You are English?" the taller of the police asked.

"I am American."

Sage was now seated on top of her assailant. He produced something that looked like a badge, and one of the policemen glanced at it.

"We all go to the station. You can tell us your story there," one of the cops said, taking her arm.

Another boat bearing more cops pulled up and they all got in. Vivianne was finally able to get a good look at the thug who had attempted to assault her. In the scuffle, he had lost his sunglasses and he sat, eyes lowered, muttering to himself in Italian.

A short ride and a brisk walk later, they arrived at the station. With the aid of an interpreter, they finally got the mess sorted out. Vivianne told the police about all the incidents leading up to today. She was forced to show her identification and was surprised when her name did not produce the usual grimace. Vivianne Baxter didn't seem to matter here.

The policemen simply shrugged after scrutinizing Sage's FBI credentials. They didn't seem overly impressed. Vivianne didn't even want to guess why Sage still had his badge. She surmised it was what probably had spared them a more intense interrogation.

Her attacker, after being pressed, admitted his name was Vincenzo. He had a long criminal record for petty thefts, and admitted he'd been hired to find Vivianne by his boss, a man called Guido. He was booked and transported by boat to jail. After giving the address of their hotel, Sage and Vivianne were free to go.

The streets were practically empty when they left the precinct. A few bleary-eyed shopkeepers peered out disinterestedly from inside their stores.

"How are you holding up?" Sage asked, placing an arm around her shoulders. "So far Venice hasn't been much fun."

Vivianne began to tremble, and the tears she'd held back started to flow. It finally sunk in, what she'd been through.

"Come sit for a while," Sage said, leading her into a café and ordering them both Campari and soda.

While they waited for their drinks to be served, Vivianne blew her nose loudly and tried pulling herself together.

"I'm still trying to make sense of this," she sniffled. "Who would hire these men to abduct me?"

"Think," Sage said, handing her a crisp white handkerchief from his pocket. "Maybe this has to do with your previous job. Is there something you know that you haven't told me?"

Sage's cell phone jingled. He looked at the dial and debated whether to answer.

"Shouldn't you get that?" Vivianne asked when the ringing persisted.

Sage grimaced. "It's Stan and Nona Gabriel. I have no idea what to say to them."

"You'll come up with something."

He punched a button and barked, "Hello."

Vivianne could hear Nona Gabriel's voice loud and clear. "Sage, Stan and I are calling for our daily update. He's on the extension."

"Uh, we're still in Venice," Sage said.

"You were supposed to be in Rome. Why aren't you there?"

"We had a bit of a problem. Our departure's been delayed."

"What's wrong?" Stan interjected in the unmistakable baritone he'd become famous for.

"A few minor glitches but we're working it out."

"Maya's not in trouble?" Stan asked.

There was a momentary hesitation before Sage responded. "Maya's fine."

"She hasn't gotten involved with some unsavory character?" The question came from Nona, who sounded like she wanted to cry.

Alec, Vivianne supposed, could be labeled an unsavory character, at least by the Gabriels' standards. Alec's appearance alone would put them off. That plus the fact that he was a student with no money to speak of.

"Sage? Tell me Maya hasn't done something stupid," Nona's worried tones insisted.

"Not that I know of."

That wasn't a complete lie. Sage hadn't a clue what Maya was up to, but stupid she was not.

"Okay, we'll call tomorrow. By then you should be in Rome, right?"

"I'll let you know if that doesn't materialize," Sage said, hanging up. He downed his Campari and soda. "Time to head back to the hotel," he said.

She was up and standing beside him. When he hugged

her, she held on to him with all the strength she could muster. They needed each other. Sage was the only one she could trust.

Nine

Todd Aikens glared at Harold Huggins, who sat across from him. "I can't believe you're passing me over after all we've been through."

Harold swiveled his expensive burgundy leather chair, faced Todd, and returned his glare. "I'm not passing you over. Your time hasn't come. Excuse me," he said, picking up his phone.

Todd thumped a closed fist on the desk. "Your response isn't good enough, I demand an explanation."

"You're not management material, Todd."

How dare Harold say this to him? Todd pounded both fists on the expensive mahogany desk. His beefy boss scooted back, putting a safe distance between them. The desk provided a barrier, one that Todd would gladly hurdle.

"Funny, you didn't think so a few months back," Todd yelled. "You said if I helped you get rid of Vivianne Baxter I would be rewarded. Time to deliver, Harold."

Harold slammed the receiver back into its cradle. "That was then. This is now. You're hardly a shining star."

"I went out on a limb for you," Todd sputtered. "I lied—"

Harold held a hand up, backing him off. "There isn't anything left to discuss. Please show yourself out."

"Like hell, there isn't," Todd yelled, standing. "Vivianne Baxter doesn't work here anymore, and all because of you."

"Keep your voice down. Lest you forget, you played a major part in Vivianne's dismissal."

Todd felt his cheeks flush. Harold had promised him that once he got Vivianne's job he would give him the supervisor's slot. Now he'd forgotten his promise. Instead he'd promoted Bill Wright to the coveted position. Bill now sat in the corner office while Todd remained in his cubicle.

"You haven't heard the last of this," Todd said, stabbing a finger at Harold. "If you push me . . . I'll . . ."

"You'll what?"

Harold pressed the intercom button. His large vein-streaked jowls shook. "Don't even think about threatening me."

"I'll . . . I'll go to Kathryn Samuels and tell her the whole truth."

"You wouldn't dare. You'd implicate yourself."

"Try me."

Harold turned icy-cold blue eyes on Todd. "If another supervisor's slot opens up you'll be given a shot. I have work to do and so do you."

More empty promises. Nothing would materialize. Harold was not to be trusted. He'd disliked working for Vivianne Baxter, simply because she was a woman. He'd made her life miserable, and he'd accused her of sexual harassment. Todd had supported Harold, even though he knew he'd lied. Todd had nothing personal against Vivianne; she simply stood in the way of advancement.

The whole thing had started off innocently enough, diverting a few checks here and there, donations that were not easily traceable. Confident that they would not be discovered, he, Harold, and Bill had grown increasingly bold. Vivianne had been the one to intercept the calls when two organizations had not received confirmation of their contributions. In actuality there had been many more.

When Vivianne had walked in on a conversation she

should never have heard, Harold panicked. Fearing for their jobs and reputation, Harold had come up with the elaborate scheme to get rid of Vivianne. Todd and Bill had gone along.

Initially, Todd had been upset; he hated to lie. Vivianne had always been nice to him. She was tough as nails when business required it, but she'd been warm and affectionate to her staff. She never forgot a birthday and would bake beautiful cakes. She'd also been kind and considerate.

Todd remembered how she'd given him time off when his wife was sick. Then she'd baked cookies and mailed them to his home. But Vivianne would have shown little compassion if she'd confirmed they were stealing. She was a company person through and through.

"I've got a meeting," Harold said, rising. He spoke into the intercom. "Betty, Mr. Aikens is about to leave, he needs an appointment with me." Setting down the receiver, he punched Todd's arm playfully. "We'll talk more later."

Later would never happen, Todd knew that. Harold would do just about anything to avoid him. "I'll arrange things with Betty, then," Todd said, heading for the door.

Betty was Harold's recently promoted secretary. It was rumored that the two were having an affair. The buxom blonde guarded Harold better than any Foo Dog could.

With a wave of Harold's beefy hand, Todd was dismissed. He walked out of Harold's spacious office angrier than he'd ever been. He'd bragged to his colleagues that he would be sitting in the corner office, and he'd already spent the money that came with a big fat raise.

Todd stopped at Betty's desk. She smiled at him vacuously, painted nails pecking at the keyboard of her computer.

"Todd," she said, giving him an eyeful of cleavage, "Har says you need time on his calendar. Let me see what I can do." She clicked her mouse, bringing up Harold's calendar, and then made an exaggerated grimace. "The next three weeks are booked, I'm afraid."

"I need to see Harold sooner than that," Todd said, smiling at the woman he'd privately labeled a bimbo. She was free with her favors and everyone knew it.

Betty sighed loudly. "Can't do." She barely hid her gleeful expression.

Todd placed his butt on the edge of her desk. "Try harder, Betty. There's got to be something."

Betty crossed her arms, her huge breasts spilled over the top of her dress. "Har's totally booked."

"Unbook him," Todd said, leaning over and swiveling the monitor his way. He stabbed a finger at an open spot. "There's an opening at two on Friday."

Betty's eyes went round, she sputtered. "I left that slot open. Har has a business lunch."

Todd jabbed his finger at another open spot. "What about ten o'clock on Thursday?"

"Har's coming in late that day."

Todd made up his mind then. He would go directly to the board with his story, if that's what it took. He'd lied before and could lie again. He would say that he'd been forced to support Harold's story. He'd been threatened with losing his job. He was sick to death of sitting in that cubicle while Harold and Bill called the shots.

Todd tried one last time. "Look," he said to Betty, "talk to Harold and tell him I'll need to be seen this week. If I don't get an appointment I'm going over his head. Be sure to tell him that."

Betty stared openly as Todd walked away.

Maya felt wonderful, better than wonderful. Alec had been a skillful lover, and so patient with her. It was too early to tell him that she was in love with him. But she was. He hadn't said the words she hoped to hear, but that didn't matter. He couldn't make love to her that way, and not feel.

She rested her head against his shoulders as they strolled hand in hand across the Ponte Rialto, Alec occasionally referring to his guidebook. He told her that the stone bridge they crossed had replaced an earlier wooden version. The best architects had vied for the job, which had eventually gone to Antonio da Ponte because he was able to keep costs down, and at a time when the republic most needed it.

A golden light cast an awesome hue on the rippling waters of the Grand Canal. Gondolas and speedboats zipped by carrying locals and lovers. The side paths were filled with people strolling and chatting. Maya wanted to pinch herself. In her wildest dreams she had never imagined she would be walking over a bridge in Venice with a man she loved.

She refused to acknowledge the twinge of guilt that had surfaced. Her parents would die if they knew she was hanging out with Alec, much less sleeping with him. They would have labeled him totally unsuitable, and truth was, in many ways he was. Alec had neither polish nor money, but he was young and ambitious, and listened to her. Really listened.

"Alec," Maya said, "are you an only child?"

The question seemed to catch him by surprise. He blinked at her, and tossed a lock out of one eye. He seldom talked about his family. "I have a little sister. She's fifteen and quite the thing," he said.

His tone seemed kinder, gentler now.

"And her name is?"

"Trina. My mother married briefly when I was five."

"Then you have a stepfather?"

"Had," he said, his voice turning gruff. "He left my mother two years after she had Trina."

"So basically your mother raised two children all on her own."

"Yes. She's a remarkable woman. She's had a hard life but never became sour. I got my tenacity from her. I also learned not to get too attached; that way you're never disappointed when your lovers move on."

He was sending her a message, loud and clear. Don't get too attached. What they'd shared was purely sex, while for her it had been so much more.

Maya blinked back tears. She wanted to ask him if their lovemaking meant nothing to him, but a little voice cautioned, *Take it easy. Don't scare him away.*

"I take it you speak from experience," she said.

He grunted. "Do you know what it's like to grow up without a father? When my mother got pregnant he disappeared. Later, I saw my mother go into a funk after her husband left. After that I swore off making the mistake of ever falling in love."

Maya's stomach felt as if someone had stomped on it. Alec had quickly put an end to any romantic notions she might have.

"What about your girlfriends? Did you have bad experiences with them?"

What a glutton for punishment she was.

"I never got serious so it didn't matter."

Warning number two. *Don't get serious about me.*

"Not even one of them meant anything to you?"

"Love is a wasted emotion," Alec said.

Maya had the sinking feeling that she was being used. She was here with him because she was convenient.

"But you're twenty-two, you must have cared for at least one of them," she insisted.

He chuckled, an ugly sound. "If one of those girls even got that notion, I lost them quick."

His words seemed so harsh. Final. The arm Alec had casually thrown over her shoulder felt like a weight. She slid out from under him and he leaned over the bridge, looking down into the darkening water, careful to maintain a distance, fearful to even have their shoulders touch. Anxiety filled her—loving Alec was going to hurt.

"Alec," she began tentatively, "I mean nothing to you?"

He cast her a tawny-eyed glance. "Let's get something straight. I'm digging you all right, but my goal is to graduate from college and get a job so that I can pursue my art. I can't afford distractions."

His words pierced her. But in fairness to him he hadn't made promises. She'd chosen to stay in Venice of her own free will and he hadn't forced her to make love with him.

She threw an arm around his neck and kissed his cheek. "Hey, we aren't talking lifetime commitments here. We're having fun. I like you, Alec, and I thought you liked me."

"I do. I'm hungry. Let's scope out a place to eat."

The conversation had ended abruptly. Best not to push him for more.

Alec took her hand and Maya's heart did a rapid pitter-pat. Regardless of what he said, he seemed to want to be with her. She'd give it time. Somehow she would make Alec fall in love with her.

Sage and Vivianne entered the cool lobby of the Hespario and approached the desk. A bespectacled young man waved them over.

"Do you need a room?" he asked.

Sage stepped forward. "No. We're here to meet friends."

"Their names, please."

"Maya Gabriel and Alec Randolf."

The clerk pursed his lips. "No one by those names has checked in."

"But you haven't even looked," Vivianne said, asserting herself.

The clerk removed his glasses, wiping them with the

edges of a handkerchief. "I don't need to. I know everyone that is registered."

"Can you at least check?" Sage insisted.

The man shrugged. *"Bene."* He began thumbing through a voluminous ledger and then turned back. "They are not here."

"Let's try the Bernardi Semenzato," Vivianne said, taking Sage's arm and moving him along. She could tell from the set of his shoulders that he was wired. It had been a long, grueling day.

"By the way," he said, "I forgot to mention that you look quite beautiful tonight."

Sage's words warmed Vivianne all over. She had taken time with her appearance, forgoing the usual black.

"Thank you," she managed.

Since the tour group had moved on to Rome, Vivianne had given up trying to hide. This evening she wore a lavender sundress with a black shawl stylishly draped over one shoulder. She'd accessorized the outfit with silver earrings and a bracelet. Her efforts had not been missed by Sage. His tongue had practically hung to the floor when she'd appeared in the Metropole's lobby.

They boarded a water bus and headed for the Bernardi Semenzato. Spotting the building, Vivianne said, "The woman at the Metropole said it was cheap?"

Sage held the entrance door open for Vivianne. "Money isn't exactly a problem for Maya, lest you forget."

"It is for Alec. Proud as he is, I can't imagine him accepting a handout from a woman."

"That's what you think," Sage muttered, pausing before a seated area off to the side.

"What's that supposed to mean?"

"I checked out his background. He has a history of taking up with young girls with money."

Vivianne gasped and sank onto one of the overstuffed

chairs. "I would never have guessed." Sage joined her.

"Alec Randolf is a player," he continued. "Most likely he found out who Maya's parents are; that's why he latched on to her."

Vivianne didn't want to believe it. She liked Alec, grumpy as he was. But who wouldn't be grumpy when you always had an unwanted third wheel, and a fourth if she included herself?

"It's more like Maya latched on to him," Vivianne said, thinking about it.

"Okay. They latched on to each other. Still, I have a responsibility to the Gabriels. I'm here in Venice because they pay me a good salary to look after their daughter. And I failed."

"You did not," Vivianne said, taking his hand. "You've done a good job so far. How could you predict that Maya would run off with Alec? And even if you had, how could you possibly have stopped them?"

"By force if need be, and if necessary, I could have told Maya that I was a hired bodyguard. I could have threatened to call her parents."

"Maya is twenty years old. Do you recall being twenty years old?" Vivianne asked wryly.

Sage flashed back an equally wry grin. Vivianne's stomach flip-flopped and tiny goose bumps broke out on her arms. Why did he have to be so attractive? And why did she have to feel something for him?

"Twenty seems a long time back," Sage said, "but yes, I remember I was so full of myself."

"And no one could stop you from doing what you wanted to. If they tried you simply rebelled."

"Yes, but this is different. I wasn't some spoiled rich kid with assets to worry about."

"Wealth and loneliness often go hand in hand. Maya likes Alec because he's down-to-earth with few pretensions.

Maybe she's looking for a little companionship. Someone who accepts her the way she is."

"Could be, but that boy's history worries me."

Sage took her hand. The warmth of his palm produced a tingly feeling. He smelled like raw male and his musky cologne emphasized that fact. Unaware of the electric connection, Sage seemed distracted. He was hell-bent on finding Maya and Alec. Nothing else mattered until that happened.

This evening he wore one of his trademark polo shirts, leaving the strong column of his neck exposed. His bulging biceps and washboard stomach were what women fantasized about. He was a man who clearly worked out.

Stop the X-rated thoughts. Stop them.

They started toward the front desk, where a number of tourists were milling around.

"We're here to see Alec Randolf and Maya Gabriel," Sage said, presenting himself. "Could you ring their room please?"

The woman at the front desk smiled pleasantly and picked up the phone. Sage's entire body relaxed as he waited for an answer.

"No one's picking up," the clerk said, after interminable seconds had passed.

At last they'd gotten confirmation that Alec and Maya were there.

"When was the last time you saw them?" Sage asked.

The clerk frowned and made an expansive gesture. "The *bella signora* and the man with the hair left earlier this afternoon. By now they should have returned."

"We'll wait then," Sage said, pointing to the sitting area. "Right over there. If you spot them, don't let on. We want to surprise them."

The clerk nodded and beckoned to the next guest in line.

Vivianne flopped into a chair with a clear view of the

hotel's entrance. Alec and Maya would be inside the building before they caught on.

Her stomach made a rumbling sound. She hoped Sage didn't hear.

He tssked sympathetically. "You're hungry. I'd like to feed you but I'm not moving until those two walk in. Grab a bite in the restaurant if you'd like."

Hungry as she was, Vivianne didn't want to leave. She couldn't risk missing the showdown. Food could be eaten at any time.

Ten

"I can't help it. I just have the feeling something's wrong. Sage sounded weird," Nona Gabriel said, setting her cosmopolitan down on a nearby table. With a worried expression, she turned to her husband.

The library was one of her favorite places, and in fact had made her want this house, high in the Hollywood hills. Enormous French doors opened onto an attractive garden that Nona tended with the aid of two Mexican gardeners. Chinese-red walls were tempered by cream moldings, and big comfortable chairs were haphazardly arranged in groupings. Books spilled from customized shelves, and a cavernous unlit fireplace took up one wall.

Stan, busy memorizing lines for his next film, merely grunted. He was used to her agonizing, she supposed. After twenty-five years of marriage, it no longer bothered her that he listened with one ear. She knew he had a tendency to compartmentalize, and right now he was focused on his work, but she was bound and determined to get his attention.

Nona approached, waving a manicured hand in front of Stan's face. "Put down that stupid script and listen to me," she screeched, getting into his face. "My motherly intuition tells me that Maya's in trouble and you're so absorbed in that blasted thing you don't even care."

That got Stan's attention. He gazed at her warily but she knew he was still not present.

"Frankly, sweetheart," he muttered, "I couldn't care less."

"You don't care that your only daughter might be in trouble?" Nona railed. "She's your pride and joy, the thing you love more than life itself!"

Stan had the grace to look shamefaced. "Sorry," he said. "I was memorizing my lines, of course I love Maya."

"I have a mind to call Sage again," Nona said, flipping open her cell phone.

"What, at this hour? The man's bound to think you're mad." An ebony arm whipped out, retrieving the cell phone. Stan pocketed it. "You can call him tomorrow."

Nona bit back a curse. "Now why did you do that? How am I supposed to sleep when I know there's something the matter with my baby girl?"

"You won't sleep because of the four cosmopolitans you've drunk. That has nothing to do with Maya."

"I had three cocktails, hardly enough to give me a buzz." Nona glared at her husband and retrieved her abandoned drink. She sipped on it and said, "If any harm comes to my child, I'm going to have that man drawn and quartered."

"That man's name is Sage and we're paying him plenty to keep that child safe. Now will you chill?" Stan kept his eye on his script.

"I'll chill when Sage can assure me that Maya hasn't been out of his sight. I'll chill when Maya calls me and I can speak with her. We haven't heard from her in several days."

"That's hardly unusual," Stan said in a voice that indicated he'd had enough. "In case you forget, Maya took this trip to assert her independence, and so far she has managed quite well."

Stan focused his attention on the manuscript he clutched.

"There you go again," Nona cried, snatching the script away and tossing it onto one of the Queen Anne chairs. "I'm upset, and you're not doing a thing to comfort me."

Stan rolled his eyes. "Such hysterics."

The cell phone in his pocket rang. Nona dove to retrieve it. In her haste she almost ripped Stan's shirt.

"Easy," he said, delving into his pocket, producing the phone, and hitting the yes button. "Hello."

Nona could tell by his stilted responses that it wasn't the call she hoped for. Stan rolled his eyes and held the phone out to her, mouthing "Gwen."

Gwen was her best friend and a fellow actor. Nona accepted the call and began speaking rapidly. Gwen would understand, she had a child Maya's age, one that had given her premature gray hairs.

Tomorrow she would pin Sage down. If she didn't like his answers she would call the Buena Vista group herself and find out where Maya was. Then she would book a flight. She would do anything to bring her baby back home.

Alec and Maya had consumed two bottles of wine at the restaurant and were feeling no pain. Unsteadily, they wended their way back to the hotel.

The place had been a find, serving food that was cheap and plentiful. It had been filled with locals, a good sign. A violinist roamed, stopping by each table, taking requests. Alec had requested *"La Sola Mia,"* a song Maya enjoyed. The conversation was upbeat and light, just like he liked it.

When Maya's steps faltered, Alec placed an arm around her and nuzzled her cheek. He liked playing a protective role, and Maya needed protecting.

A Roman candle lit up the sky, coating it shimmering pinks and golds. When they stopped to admire the colorful display, Maya clapped and twirled, her long skirt billowing about her.

"Oh, let's not go back just yet," she said. "Let's walk and see where we end up."

Against his better judgment, Alec agreed. They'd both

had too much to drink and bed seemed the safest place to be. But he was enjoying himself, being with Maya felt good.

"Where to, then?" Alec asked.

"St. Mark's Square. I'd love to see it at night."

"St. Mark's Square it is."

Maya skipped ahead of him. Alec made sure to keep an eye on her. They were not the only ones roaming the streets at this late hour, and an attractive woman who'd had too much to drink was asking for trouble. They trailed a group of inebriated tourists through winding alleys and over cobblestone bridges, following the signs for St. Mark's Square.

Street musicians played on every corner, upturned hats and open guitar cases indicating that tips would be welcomed. Alec occasionally contributed a coin. While he needed every dime, struggling artists needed it more. He'd never resort to soliciting, but one needed to do what one needed to do.

In St. Mark's Square, flashbulbs exploded as couples posed for photographs. A sizable crowd sat at an outdoor café, sipping after-dinner liqueurs or the strong, sweet espressos that could become addictive.

"Cappuccino?" Alec suggested, thinking that walking into the lobby of the hotel looking and smelling as if they had consumed a brewery wasn't a good idea.

"Okay," Maya said, "but I don't want to sit, let's grab a couple of cups from the vendor over there." She pointed to a man with a cart and a long line of people, and headed off.

Alec shook his head. No point in stopping her. He'd never met a woman so uninhibited, or so unaware of her looks. Maya operated on pure instinct. She made love with wild abandon, with more enthusiasm than form. Still, he enjoyed every moment he spent with her, but things needed to be kept in perspective. They were on vacation and in a week or so would go their separate ways.

When it came their turn, Maya purchased two cups of cappuccino and handed one to Alec. Carrying their disposable cups, they walked toward the Bacino di San Marco, where excursion boats were moored to the dock. They practically had the place to themselves.

This was the grand entrance to the Republic, Alec had been told. St. Theodore, the first patron saint of Venice, and his dragon guarded one column. A winged lion guarded the other. It was no wonder that when Napoleon and his troops arrived in Venice he'd called the Piazza San Marco the world's most beautiful drawing room.

The smell of brine in his nostrils, Alec listened to the waves lapping against the pilings. A pitch-black sky above gave the illusion he'd been thrown back in time. He closed his eyes, imprinting the scene on his mind, wishing he had his sketchbook. Maya sat quietly on the dock, her feet dangling over the sides. In a moment he would join her.

Out here it was difficult to remember what life was like in Brooklyn. And he couldn't simply forget the goals he'd set for himself. A girl from the West Coast, sweet as she was, was simply not part of the plan.

Maya wiggled her toes and finished the last drop of cappuccino. "Oh, Alec, isn't this cool?" she said, throwing her arms around his neck and kissing him.

He kissed her back, liking the feel of her arms around his neck, inhaling the scent that was uniquely Maya's. Her body was lush, her skin smooth. Maybe it was the wine they'd consumed that made him feel as if he were on top of the world, or was it her kiss that had him spinning out of control? It was the best he'd ever experienced: deep, soulful, and filled with promise.

Still, there were things about Maya he did not know, like where she lived or even where she went to school. He'd helped carry her smart Louis Vuitton luggage, balancing his knapsack with his raggedy clothing on one shoulder. Most students could not afford such bags. Then again, most students weren't Maya.

"Did you tell your parents you've decided to stay on in Venice?" Alec asked.

Maya fidgeted. "Actually, no. I didn't think it was necessary."

"Why not?" he demanded.

"Because they would ask who I was staying with and I would be forced to lie."

He narrowed his eyes and squinted at her. "Are you ashamed that we're together?"

There was his insecurity kicking in, fear that he would not measure up, that someone from Maya's social background wouldn't take him seriously, that he would be regarded as a toy to be used and discarded. He'd dated wealthy girls before, but never got too involved. Dating Maya would be asking for trouble.

"Why would I be ashamed of you?" Maya asked, her voice sounding reed-thin. "My parents are overprotective and anyone interested in me is suspect, even if it were Samuel Jackson's son."

"You're hardly a child," Alec answered. "In a few months you'll be twenty-one." Maya had told him that her birthday was in September. "How will you handle it when your parents discover you're not in Rome?"

Maya shrugged and skirted the question. "What about your mother? Did you call and tell her you'd decided to stay in Venice?"

"Don't have to. I'm a big boy."

Alec hadn't spoken to his mother since arriving in Europe. She wasn't the type to worry and knew that he could take care of himself. He always had and always would.

"Maya," he said, "I saw the travelers checks on your dresser. There must be thousands of dollars there, more money than my part-time job pays me in a year. You used a gold American Express card to pay for dinner, what's up with that?"

"It's my money," Maya said defensively. "Money I saved. I've had that American Express card forever."

Alec didn't doubt that it was her money and her American Express card. Still, most girls her age didn't have access to unlimited spending.

He gazed at her warily, an uncomfortable thought formulating. "You said your parents were businesspeople—have they always indulged you like this?"

"I'm not pampered and spoiled, if that's what you're implying," Maya said, getting to her feet. "I'm not, you know. What I am is tired. I want to go back to the hotel."

"Then we'll go."

Alec tried to take Maya's hand but she pulled away. She remained distant and aloof as they walked back. His prying had brought about this change of mood, and he had the uncomfortable feeling she wasn't being open and honest with him. He'd wait until she fell asleep to go through her things. Depending on what he discovered, he'd decide whether to move on or not.

It was well after midnight, and still no sign of the missing couple. Vivianne had fallen asleep in her chair and they still hadn't eaten. Guilt forced Sage to wake her up. There was really no point in sitting there waiting. Tomorrow he'd return early, when there was a better chance of catching Alec and Maya asleep.

Sage tapped Vivianne lightly on the arm. "Okay, sleepyhead, let's go."

Vivianne yawned and squinted at him. "How long have I been asleep?" she asked.

"A little over an hour."

"An hour?" She looked horrified. "I take it Alec and Maya didn't show up?"

Sage shook his head. "Not that I know of. I'm going to check with the front desk one last time, and see if there's a back entrance. I'll have the clerk call the room again."

The sleepy-eyed receptionist seemed baffled when they approached. "I didn't realize you were still here," she said.

"Please ring Alec Randolf's room one last time," Sage requested.

The clerk picked up the phone, dialed, then shook her head. "No one's answering."

"Is there another entrance?" Sage asked.

"Just a door the staff uses."

"Please call us a water taxi, then."

Reluctant as he was to leave, Sage acknowledged he was exhausted. It had been a long, stressful day. He was starving and he doubted anything would be open this late, not even room service. But at least he could offer Vivianne a snack. He did have a loaf of bread in his room, purchased earlier from one of the shops, and he did have cheese, wine and fruit.

They started back through empty streets, making their way to the landing dock where the taxi was already waiting. The driver seemed in a hurry to go and once they sat down the boat started up.

Vivianne yawned again. Sage placed his arm around her and drew her head against his shoulder. She snuggled into him. At least he'd accomplished something today. One of the men who'd accosted Vivianne had been arrested and they'd found out where Maya and Alec were staying. Tomorrow, as soon as he found Maya, they would be on their way to Rome.

Eleven

Maya, still fully clothed, was dead asleep. She snored softly as Alec slid from beneath the covers and tiptoed to the closet. Opening the doors, he stepped into the spacious interior and snapped on the light. Maya's pricey Vuitton luggage was in the corner, garments and accessories spilling over the sides.

Alec picked up both pieces of luggage and took a seat on the floor. He was about to do the unthinkable, rummage through Maya's personal items, and God knew what he would find.

He justified his actions by reasoning that he'd tried asking Maya about herself but she'd evaded his questions. What choice did he have but to do this? He raised the lid on the suitcase and items came flying out at him: clothes, shoes and toiletries, more than his mother and sister had combined.

Fascinated by the materials of silks, satins, and linens, he picked up a shirt, held it to his nose, and inhaled. Eau de Maya filled all his senses and hurled him into a state of confusion. He tossed the blouse aside as if it were poison. He was on a mission and couldn't afford to be distracted.

Alec's fingers closed around velvet pouches holding trinkets Maya had bought: Murano glass animals, beaded jewelry, a cameo or two. She did have impeccable taste. Expensive taste. He stacked embroidered shawls, skirts, and slacks into piles and examined lotions and perfumes bearing names like Dior and Tiffany. Even the wealthy girls he'd dated didn't have half of this stuff.

When he got to the bottom of the suitcase where a black leather coat lay folded, he riffled through the pockets, removing a package of tissues, loose change, and gum. A little leather book got his attention. He palmed it and sat cross-legged, flipped through pages filled with names like Washington, Williams, Perez, Lee, and Berry. Could they be *the* Spike Lee and Halle Berry? If so, Maya moved in rather impressive circles.

Putting the book aside, Alec dug through Maya's matching tote, his fingers closing around an acrylic object that was a picture frame. He removed the item and gazed at the photo. A familiar couple stared back. He'd seen their faces on the covers of magazines like *Ebony* and *Essence, Entertainment Weekly,* and such. Nona and Stan Gabriel were two of Hollywood's most respected and sought-after black box office draws.

The realization of his discovery ricocheted through Alec, causing him to almost drop the picture frame. Maya was Stan and Nona's daughter. Why had she kept that a secret from him? Clutching the photo, he tiptoed out of the closet and crossed over to the dresser where Maya's travelers checks lay. He sorted the checks into denominations and began thumbing through them, counting slowly. One thousand, two thousand. Easily eight thousand dollars. He never even heard Maya approach.

"What do you think you're doing?" she hissed, holding her hand out. "Give them to me."

Though she was bleary-eyed, Alec could tell she was furious, and rightly so. He stared at her, unable to find words to offer an explanation. Handing the checks over he forced himself to say, "I—"

She was on him in a flash. "You what? Got caught red-handed stealing my stuff? You waited until I was asleep to search through my things." She snatched the photo out of his hand. "You invaded my privacy."

How could he explain his actions? Maya would never understand. He'd been caught snooping and she'd assumed the worst. He wanted to hold her, comfort her, to make the tears streaming down her face disappear. Instead, he stood immobile as she walked into the open closet and began stuffing her things haphazardly into bags. Somehow he had to find words to make her understand that it wasn't the way it looked. That he'd only been consumed by curiosity and wanted to know who she was.

"Look, Maya," Alec said, finally finding his tongue, "you weren't very open. You never spoke about your family. You had expensive things and seemed to have lots of money. I thought if I searched through your stuff I might find some clue."

"Sure you did," Maya yelled back. "And what were my travelers checks supposed to tell you? You were caught counting my money, for God's sake. You would have been long gone if I hadn't woken up."

She was calling him a thief and he resented that.

"If the shoe were on the other foot, what would you do?" he shouted at her. "Do you think I'm happy finding out that you've been slumming, playing me?"

"I was not playing you, Alec. I was enjoying your company. Is that so difficult to believe?"

"What would a daughter of movie stars want with someone like me?"

Maya's face went soft, then hardened again. "Maybe I like the fact that you're down-to-earth and straightforward," she continued brusquely. "I never imagined that you were a thief."

"I am not. I may not have the cheese but at least I am not ashamed of who I am."

"Cheese? What's cheese?"

"Money."

"And money is important to you. I think you knew all along who my parents were, that's why you befriended me. You used me, Alec."

It hurt that she thought so little of him. Granted, he hadn't wanted things to get serious, but he'd never led her on, he'd told her from the beginning he didn't want to get attached.

"I hooked up with you because I like you," Alec admitted. "You were fun."

He tried taking her arm but Maya shrugged him off. Tears still streaming down her face, she stepped into sweats and grabbed her purse. She pulled her suitcase and tote from the closet and stomped to the door. Alec followed behind her. He couldn't let her go out in her current state.

"Wait," he said. "What do you think you're doing?"

"Leaving. Going away from this place."

"Not at this hour. It's late. Tomorrow I'll help you find another hotel, or catch up with the group, if that's what you want."

"I'm not spending another second here. I can't stand you," she screamed.

Alec reached for her arm.

Maya tugged away. "Let go of me."

She yanked the door open.

Alec tried one last time. "Maya, it's not safe going out on your own. You've got tourist written all over your face. You have luggage and no place to stay."

Stony-faced, Maya turned back to him. "Get this straight, Alec. I never want to see you again."

The door slammed shut behind her.

"I feel awful," Sage said, as he and Vivianne entered the Metropole's deserted lobby. "You still haven't eaten."

"That was my choice. I could have gone to the restaurant as you suggested. I'll survive."

He debated for a moment before extending the invitation. "I have snacks in my room if you'd like to come up."

Vivianne seemed to contemplate before making up her mind. "Okay, anything's better than going to bed with a rumbling stomach," she said, taking his hand.

"We can't have you do that."

Vivianne's lovely sundress was all wrinkled. The scarf that had been stylishly thrown over one shoulder was now wrapped around her neck. But even in her sleepy-eyed state, she was beautiful. Beautiful and tempting.

"I didn't mean to sound ungrateful," Vivianne said, following Sage off the elevator and down the long hallway.

"You didn't. How do bread, cheese, and fruit sound?"

"Like a feast. You're a lifesaver." Impulsively, she kissed his cheek.

"And there's wine," Sage said, holding the door open before he lost it altogether.

Vivianne stepped into the room and he snapped on the lights. The place had been picked up by the maid and the clothes he'd hastily stepped out of were hung, and the bed made. Sage gestured to the comfortable art deco couch. "Have a seat. Make yourself comfortable."

She sat, kicked off sandals, and massaged what must have been aching feet.

Sage buried his face in the refrigerator. The sight of all that leg had his heart pounding and his engines revved. He retrieved the promised fare and set bread, cheese, and fruit on the table, then got busy opening the wine.

"I don't have napkins," he apologized, tossing Vivianne a washcloth retrieved from the bathroom.

She laid her head back on the couch; one hand circled the wine goblet. "It's been a tough day."

"Yes, it's been rough."

Sage came to sit beside her. He slipped out of his loafers and flexed his legs.

Vivianne wiggled hot-pink toenails and said, "Here's to finding Maya tomorrow." She clinked her glass against his. "Where's that food?"

"In front of you."

There was a contented expression on her face as she gobbled the snack. He much preferred to watch her but satisfied himself by popping a handful of grapes into his mouth. Tomorrow he would deal with Maya and Alec. Randolf had probably already taken advantage of Maya. And it was all his fault, because he'd allowed himself to become distracted by Vivianne. He deserved to have his ears boxed.

It was a disquieting thought that he could so easily lose focus. There had been a time in his life when work had been all-consuming, and relationships took a backseat. It made him a poor choice for any woman wanting a commitment. His ex-wife had told him so, justifying why she too had buried herself in work and found solace with another.

He didn't want to think about her. Determined not to become maudlin, Sage turned the radio on. A soft Italian ballad filled the room. He topped off their wineglasses and sat back.

"I really should go to my room," Vivianne said after a while. "But the truth is, I'm afraid to be alone."

Her confession surprised him. She'd seemed strong through it all, demonstrating remarkable composure. He wanted to hug her to him and wipe away her fears.

"You think someone might be lurking in your room?" Sage asked.

Vivianne's hand massaged her forehead. "Anything's possible. Look at what happened earlier today."

An idea began to formulate. One Sage quickly dismissed. The scent of Vivianne's perfume, a heady spring breeze, titillated his nostrils. To heck with caution, he decided. What if he invited her to stay?

Sage knew he was courting trouble, playing with fire.

He'd been attracted to Vivianne from the very moment he laid eyes on her and heard her incredible voice. A voice that commanded attention, that made you sit up and listen. She'd gone through a rough time and so had he. Inviting her to stay was the least he could do.

"Spend the night with me," Sage said, crossing his fingers behind his back.

Vivianne's gaze locked with his. "I don't know."

He was lost in those eyes of hers. Sage pressed his advantage. "You said you didn't want to be alone. Nothing will happen unless we want it to."

"I don't have anything to sleep in. I don't have a toothbrush with me," Vivianne jabbered.

A lame excuse if he'd ever heard one, but she was weakening and that was a good thing.

"That's easily remedied," Sage said, getting up. "I'll walk with you to your room and wait for you to gather your things."

Ten minutes later they were back. While Vivianne excused herself to use the bathroom, Sage got ready for bed. Normally he slept naked, but tonight he slid into gym shorts and thought about putting on a T-shirt. Vivianne's appearance put an end to any thoughts of finding a shirt.

"Nice pecs," she said, flicking a finger across his chest.

Sage gaped as he eyed her attire. She wore a man's black satin pajama top that came down to her thighs. Out the door went any thoughts of sleeping tonight.

Taking a calming breath, he got under the covers and patted the spot next to him. Vivianne slid in beside him. The scent of late spring filled his nostrils and her leg brushed against his. He quickly snapped off the lamp and tried closing his eyes. Vivianne's luscious body filled his vision as he rolled onto his side and plumped up the pillows.

"Are you asleep?" Vivianne whispered, a finger poking his side.

Sage's body sprang to life. Why had she touched him?

"What's wrong?"

Vivianne's hand gently rubbed his back. "Thanks for coming to my rescue today."

"It was nothing."

He shifted and prepared to roll over.

"Not nothing. Those men could have killed me if you hadn't been there."

"Try to get some sleep," Sage muttered. *Stop touching me.*

Vivianne continued to massage his back, and predictably his lower body responded. Blood pounded in his head and throbbed at his temples. He turned on the light. Big mistake. The button on her pajama top popped. The sight of all that cinnamon flesh made him groan. He couldn't stop himself, he needed to touch her.

His index finger outlined Vivianne's clavicle. She exhaled on a deep breath. That same finger circled the hollow in her neck. Vivianne pressed a soft kiss against his mouth and he lost it. His hands circled her waist, pulling her closer. She cuddled in next to him.

Sage could feel Vivianne's breasts against his chest, feel the shallowness of her breathing. His hand reached up to claim the soft mound and his fingers circled her nipple. He grew bolder, needing to feel her, taste her, and see if she was as sweet as she smelled. He pushed the pajama shirt off her shoulder. The remaining buttons popped. Bending his lips to her breasts, he suckled one, then the other, and ran a hand over her smooth stomach. Unable to stop himself, he ventured lower, smoothing the material of the satin bikini briefs she wore.

Vivianne squirmed when his fingers eased beneath the elastic of her underpants to explore her moist opening. Her warm mouth trailed his chest, alternately lapping and nibbling at him. Sage was on fire, consumed by a powerful desire. He nipped at her neck, his hands returning to her breasts. He had to stop, find the condom in his wallet, old but serviceable, and placed it on the nightstand. He scooped her up and settled her on top of him.

The smell of spring breeze threatened to overwhelm him as he pressed Vivianne against the length of him.

"Take your shorts off," she said, her hands tugging at the elastic band at his waist.

He shifted her body so he could slide out of the confining garment, kicked his shorts across the room, and reached for her again. By then she'd shed her top and her bare breasts brushed his chest. She took him firmly in her mouth and he gasped, relishing the sensations that rushed through him.

Nothing else existed except the warmth of Vivianne's mouth and her lips holding him rigid. If she didn't stop, it would be over with prematurely. Reluctantly, he pulled away, found the foil package on the nightstand and slipped the condom on.

Sage shoved down Vivianne's underpants and straddled her. Her fingers clutched his sides and any resolve to take it nice and slow ended. When she gyrated against him, he came close to exploding. He drove into her, determined to take her over the top and make her feel what he was feeling.

"Vivianne," he said. "Oh, God, Vivianne."

"Sage, I'm almost there."

The sound of her raspy voice made him lose it. He no longer had a sense of time or place. Shooting stars erupted before his eyes, and rockets vibrated in his ears. Warm liquid gushed from him.

In a moment of clarity, he realized he loved this woman. Loved everything about her. On so many levels they bonded.

A pounding at the door brought Sage out of his euphoria. Who could be visiting at this late hour? Possibly Maya?

Sage sprang from the bed and stepped into his shorts. Vivianne scrambled into clothes and headed for the bathroom. The racket continued as he pulled a T-shirt over his head and ran to yank open the door.

"Maya."

Loud sobbing greeted him. She threw herself into his arms. "Sage," she cried. "Thank God you haven't left."

He should be elated. He'd found Maya, except her timing was bad. Really bad.

Twelve

Harold had blown Todd off again for what seemed the hundredth time, and he was damn mad. The man was avoiding him, that much was obvious. He would no longer be put off. Harold would see him or risk a scene.

Todd waited until Betty of the bosoms left for lunch, knowing that in a few minutes, Harold would follow. He stuck his head over the top of his cubicle and spotted Harold on his way out. Good, he hadn't escaped. Todd was up like a flash, blocking Harold's path.

"Harold, do you have a moment? This won't take long," Todd said, getting into his face.

Harold glanced at his watch, his face taking on a weary expression. "I'm in a rush. I've got a lunch appointment and I'm already late."

Todd had expected something like this. He brought his face even closer to Harold's. "Don't force me to make a scene."

The handful of Todd's coworkers that weren't out to lunch busily shuffled papers and pretended not to listen.

"Get out of my way," Harold said, his gruff voice carrying across the room.

Todd stood his ground. "We can talk here or in your office. Your choice."

"Talk to Betty when she gets back. Have her squeeze you in around three."

Harold glanced at his watch again, his jowls shaking with barely contained rage. Todd played his trump card. He smiled amiably. "If you prefer I can talk to Kathryn," he said.

The double rolls that were Harold's belly convulsed. His jowls shook, making a click-clacking sound. "Kathryn? What would you want with her? You need to go through channels, lad. Whatever you have to say has to be run by me. I'll give you five minutes."

Todd shot Harold another disarming smile. "I thought you'd see it my way. We'll talk *now,* then?"

Harold gulped, looking like he would much rather shove Todd out of the way. But he managed to manufacture a wintry smile. "Follow me."

He stomped back to his office, Todd trailing him. Inside, he took a seat behind the elaborate mahogany desk and examined the manicured nails of his oversize paws. "Say what you have to say."

Harold's body language was meant to intimidate. It didn't bother Todd one bit. He perched on the end of the desk, flicked imaginary lint off the breast pocket of his sports coat when in fact he was pushing the button on the mini-recorder that was concealed there. The whirring seemed awfully loud. Todd leaned across the desk, bringing his face close to Harold's.

"I want to know when I will be promoted."

"Now, now, Todd. You know these things take time."

"When?" Todd asked, his eyes never leaving Harold's face.

"I'm reorganizing the department. Something's bound to come up."

More empty promises. Another attempt to stall.

"What will that something be?" Todd asked.

Harold seemed taken aback. Todd could practically hear the wheels turning in his head. "Uh, I don't know. Didn't I mention it before? You need grooming."

The word *grooming* was what pushed Todd over the edge.

Interesting that Harold didn't think he needed grooming when they used to go to happy hours together. He hadn't thought he needed grooming when he would borrow money for lunch. And he obviously didn't need grooming when he'd lied so that Harold could have Vivianne's job.

"Harold," Todd said, looking him straight in the eye, "time to deliver. You promised me a promotion. You said I deserved it."

"I said no such thing," Harold sputtered.

"Yes, you did. I've made an appointment to speak with Kathryn Samuels. She used to be one of Vivianne's biggest champions. I plan on telling her what I know."

Harold guffawed, shaking his head. "You'd never do that. That would mean implicating yourself. We'll both be fired and what good would that do? Besides, Bill and I hired a few men to shake Vivianne up; she's traveling abroad and we can't risk her shooting off her mouth."

Todd frowned. Harold wasn't getting it.

"Why would I implicate myself?" he asked. "I was never involved in your scheme. You were the one stealing checks, I just worked for you."

A satisfied grin spread over Todd's face when he saw Harold's double chins bounce. He continued, "You told me that Vivianne was coming on to you. You said her constantly touching your arm made you uncomfortable. You asked me to keep a close eye on her. You were my manager so I did what you asked. I verified that I'd seen Vivianne call you into her office and place an arm around you. I overheard her invite you to dinner. But what did I know? You might have been the one with a crush on Vivianne. Maybe when she didn't reciprocate you turned the tables on her and cried harassment, leaving the woman to take the fall."

Harold was on his feet, practically sputtering now. His right eye twitched. "You can't repeat this garbage to Kathryn. She'd never believe you."

"Try stopping me."

Todd hoped the recorder was picking all this up.

"You're asking for trouble," Harold warned. "I know people."

"Is that a threat?"

"Call it what you want."

Todd slapped a hand against his breast, turning the machine off. He had enough on Harold.

"There's a simple solution then," he said. "Find me a management position and find it quick. I'll give you until the end of the week."

Hopping off Harold's desk, he left the man sputtering and walked out.

As soon as daylight broke, Nona called Sage. She hadn't had one wink of sleep. Her instincts told her that something was wrong with her daughter and nothing Stan had done or said reassured her otherwise.

The phone rang for an eternity before Sage picked up.

"Hello," he said, sounding irritable.

"Nona Gabriel here," she announced, getting straight to the point. "What's going on with Maya? Are you in Rome?"

"We're still in Venice," Sage said.

Nona expelled her breath with a loud whoosh. "Why aren't you in Rome? What's happened to my child?"

"There was a slight change of plans. Maya's coming home."

"What do you mean, Maya's coming home? All she talked about was going to Europe."

"That may be so, but she wants to come home and I've arranged her ticket so she can do just that."

Nona wasn't buying any of it. Maya had been excited about the trip. She'd been happy to be free of them, looking forward to asserting her independence.

"Have Maya call me immediately," Nona said briskly.

"How am I supposed to do that? She'll know we talked," Sage whispered. "She'll guess I've been retained by you."

"You're posing as her friend. Convince her to call her mother."

"Maya's mad at me," Sage admitted.

"Who's on the phone, Sage?" Maya's shrill voice interjected. "I heard you say you were retained by someone."

Sage's muffled response was lost. But at least Nona could relax; her child was alive and safe.

"What flight will Maya be on?" Nona demanded.

"Why don't you talk to her yourself?"

There was a rustle before Maya picked up, then muffled voices. It sounded as if they were arguing.

"Be reasonable," Nona was able to make out.

"Mother, is it you?" Maya asked, her voice sounding as if she hadn't slept in days.

"What's this about you coming home?" Nona started in, briskly.

Maya's heart-wrenching sobs filled the earpiece. Nona's gut constricted. It hurt to listen to her baby.

"He pretended to be my friend, when all along you'd hired him."

"Listen to me," Nona reasoned, "we begged you not to go to Europe on your own. You insisted. Sage was hired to make sure nothing went wrong."

"I'm not a child," Maya cried, "and I resent you treating me as such."

The line disconnected.

Nona redialed. This time Sage picked up.

"I'm coming to get Maya," Nona said. "Stay put until I get there."

"You'll only make things worse," Sage said. "I'll make sure she gets home safely."

Nona pursed her lips, thinking. By the time she caught a

flight to Venice Maya could be anywhere. Sage had failed them miserably, but she supposed he could be trusted to make sure Maya got home.

"Okay, but I'll need to know what flight that child is on. You can be assured Stan and I will be at the airport to take her home. After that, we'll no longer need your services. We'll pay you for your time as agreed."

"I'll be in touch with the relevant information."

Things happened for a reason. But at least Maya was coming home. That's all that Nona and Stan had ever wanted.

"That poor child's heart is broken," Vivianne said as she and Sage watched Maya go through the security checkpoint.

Maya's stance was rigid; she never looked back, didn't even stop to wave at them. The girl had been a mess, she'd spent the last two days crying.

Sage and Vivianne had taken over. They'd helped Maya with her things and despite her protests they'd come with her to the airport. She'd sat in the speedboat in stony silence, hiding behind oversize sunglasses and trying her best to ignore them.

"Yes, and she's furious with me. I violated her trust."

Vivianne let her hand linger on Sage's arm. He'd beaten himself up enough. "She's angry with me too. She thinks we're in collusion. She accused me of knowing all along that you were hired to guard her."

"The girl's in pain. Falling in love can be heartbreaking," Sage said.

Vivianne should know that. She glanced at Sage. Not one word of love had been spoken between them. He refused to meet her eyes but she could tell by the way the muscles in his jaw twitched that there had been a hidden message underlying his words. She waited quietly for him to go on. They'd slept together, but Sage had been careful to maintain emotional distance. Vivianne had taken her cue from him. She was determined to keep things in perspective. Sage hadn't seemed to want more than she was offering.

"I'm disappointed in Alec," Vivianne said, breaking the tense silence. "I would have thought he would have contacted us to at least check up on Maya."

It had taken time and a great deal of prompting to pry the story out of Maya. It was Vivianne who had handled the emotional child. Sage didn't seem to know what to do and his logical responses were not what the high-strung girl needed. No woman ever wanted to hear the man she loved was a player and was better off gone.

"Good riddance. The guy was bad to the bone," Sage said, his expression turning ugly. "I just never figured him for a small-time thief."

Vivianne linked an arm through Sage's and began leading him away. "It might just be a misunderstanding. Let's go back to the hotel."

"I'm not moving until Maya's plane takes off," Sage said, coming to an abrupt halt and almost bumping into people.

"That's all fine and good. But at least let's go outside and get some fresh air."

Standing in the tiny airport, with its poor ventilation and a barely functioning air-conditioning system, she felt as if she couldn't breathe. Half of Europe seemed to be on vacation, and people buzzed about carrying oversize hand luggage. Families were seeing loved ones off, and couples said tearful good-byes.

Once outside, Vivianne was determined to keep Sage talking. He felt that he'd fallen down on the job. He'd even suggested he travel back to Los Angeles with Maya, but she would have none of it. Maya had made it clear that if he attempted to get on the flight with her she would not go.

Vivianne was sick to death of Sage beating himself up. He'd chastised himself repeatedly for allowing Maya to hook up with Alec. He'd cursed the moments he had let Maya out of his sight and allowed his professionalism to slip. Vivianne felt responsible, she'd been the cause of his distraction.

A cool breeze blew across the water as several taxis docked. Passengers got out, carting excessive amounts of suitcases and hand luggage. Sage glanced at his watch, counting the minutes until Maya's flight was airborne. Just then a water taxi pulled in and a familiar-looking man alighted. Vivianne elbowed Sage in the gut.

"Look who's here."

Alec's dreadlocks were pulled back from his face in a ponytail. There wasn't a trace of a smile as he hefted his backpack and took purposeful strides toward the terminal.

Vivianne, seeing the determined look on Sage's face, grabbed hold of his arm. He tugged away and loped toward Alec.

"Wait up, man," Sage shouted.

Alec slowed, looked in their direction, and picked up his pace. Sage raced after him.

Vivianne tried to stave off the confrontation that would inevitably follow. Too late, Sage stood in the boy's way. Alec tried to walk around him.

"I should call the police and have you arrested," Sage said.

"What for?" Alec glared at him.

"Attempted theft, for one."

Alec's golden eyes flashed fire. "Says who? Get out of my way."

Sage jabbed a finger into Alec's chest. "Don't think about taking another step. You were caught holding Maya's checks in your hand."

"Come on, guys, enough," Vivianne said, waving her hands in the air to get their attention.

The scene drew a small crowd. Three African Americans garnered looks in Venice even when they weren't fighting.

Alec's expression turned sour. Vivianne could tell by the tightness around his mouth that he was furious.

"How have you been, Alec?" she said.

"I'd be better if he got out of my face."

Sage's finger jabbed the air. "There's a kid hurting because of you. A young woman cut short her vacation because you broke her heart. And all you were interested in was getting laid and robbing her blind."

"That's none of your business."

"Keep it civil or take it away from here," Vivianne said.

Alec hefted his knapsack and began walking away. Vivianne came alongside him. "Aren't you even going to ask how Maya is?"

"How is she?" Alec asked, reluctantly. His eyes filled briefly with pain before the familiar arrogant mask was put on. It must have taken a lot for him to ask.

"Maya's hurt and confused. She's curious to know why you did what you did. You just missed her, she's taken a flight."

"Maya cut short her vacation? She left?" He seemed dumbfounded.

Sage snorted. "That she did, and all because of you. I should break every bone in your body."

"Boys!" Vivianne shouted. "That's enough."

Cursing, Alec stomped off. "I've got a flight to catch. If you speak with Maya, tell her to call me. She has my number."

"Maya doesn't want to see you ever again," Sage said, keeping in step with him. "Vivianne told you, she's gone home."

Alec's steps floundered. His mouth worked, but nothing came out. Vivianne realized that behind all that attitude was a man who deeply cared. It seemed strange that he would try to steal from Maya. Despite their differences, they'd been good together.

Vivianne decided to take another approach. She flanked Alec. "I believe you," she said. "I believe you weren't really trying to steal travelers checks from Maya."

Alec's golden eyes flickered. "It was all a mistake. I picked up those checks because I wanted to verify that she was Stan and Nona's daughter. She imagined the worst and no amount of explaining could convince her otherwise."

Alec's story sounded plausible. It was all a big misunderstanding.

"You think we're chumps," Sage said. "Tell that garbage to someone else."

Alec's expletive was crude and to the point. He told Sage to do something that was anatomically impossible.

Vivianne thought Sage would punch the boy. She placed a restraining hand on his arm. "Stop it, you two. I'll call Maya after she gets home. I'll present your side of the story."

Alec turned one last time before entering the terminal. "Why would she believe you when she didn't believe me?"

Why indeed? But she would try, because despite all she'd been through, Vivianne still believed in love. These two young people deserved a second chance. She planned on giving it to them.

Thirteen

"I've tried reaching Sage but all I get is that blasted machine of his," Errol Powell announced. A stony-faced gathering of FBI agents silently listened as he spoke. "I've left at least a dozen messages, but he hasn't called back."

"Why would he?" Adrienne Rosario asked at last. "The guy was terminated, strong-armed out of here."

The group's hostility seared him. You could have heard a pin drop. Eyes shifted, making intimate connections. Jaw muscles twitched. It was a tough audience.

Errol had hoped to put an end to the rumors floating around about Sage by calling this briefing. He decided to try the straightforward approach.

"The agency admits it made a mistake," he said. "You all know that Tyrone Kincaid was caught red-handed snorting coke. Come to find out, everyone except me knew the guy had a problem."

"Management's always the last to know," an agent in the back row grumbled.

Tyrone had, in fact, been carted out of the building in handcuffs. With a bit of prompting, he had confessed to setting Sage up.

Difficult as it was to admit, the agency had come to the conclusion they owed Sage a huge apology. Now it was their goal to contact him and have him reinstated.

"Does anyone know of Medino's whereabouts?" Errol asked.

"I heard he was out of town," Adrienne contributed. "We've always suspected he was framed."

"Yeah, the guy lost his job," another veteran muttered.

Errol Powell had already beaten himself up. He didn't like being wrong, hated the embarrassment. Sage had been a well-respected agent. Powell rotated his shoulders, hoping the tension would ease, and charged ahead.

"Someone must know where he is."

A dozen pairs of condemning eyes focused on Errol. But no one spoke up. He used his size to intimidate, glowering at the agents, and straightened up to his full height of six feet five. It didn't make his agents twitch.

He tossed out the question, "How do we make this up to Sage?"

"You tell us," one of the rookie agents said as the others waited.

"We'll offer him back pay, for one."

"Back pay isn't good enough," Adrienne said, looking to the other agents for support.

They grunted their agreement.

Errol continued. "Tyrone has confessed to everything. He gave us a list of names of other agents that were involved."

"Yeah. Sure. And one of our better agent's been out of work all because of some guy's habit," John Sylvester, the only black agent in the room, grumbled loud enough for all to hear.

Errol threw up his hands. "Look, guys, give me a break. If you know where Sage is, you've got to speak up. I'll reinstate him on the spot. I'll kiss his ass if that's what it takes."

"You'll have to do more than that," John said. "Sage is a proud man. I don't know if he'll accept an apology. He got another job."

"What job?" Errol barked. "What do you know?"

"He's working as a bodyguard, and he's being paid quite well. The guy had to do something."

Errol snorted. "Sounds pretty lame. I can't imagine Sage holding on to that bit of fluff, when we're offering full benefits and a pension. Once an agent, always an agent. It's in the blood. Sage's family's been in law enforcement forever." Errol furrowed his brows, thinking. "A directorship's opening up shortly, he'd be in line."

John snorted. "As if he would have a shot. You might try calling his sister. She's bound to know where he is."

"Why were you holding out on me?" Errol snarled and with a wave of his hand dismissed all agents except John.

"Because it's a bitch being black."

"Don't play the race card, John. It doesn't work like that here. Just give me the sister's number."

Errol busied himself pouring coffee. "You want one?" he asked and shoved a Styrofoam cup John's way.

The agent declined. He reached over, picked up a memo pad and scrawled a number on the first clean page he found.

"That's the sister's phone number. Her name's Celeste. You'll be damn lucky if she picks up the phone."

John stood and headed for the door.

"Where are you going?" Errol bellowed.

"Out for a smoke. It's been a helluva day."

Once John was out of sight, Errol picked up the phone and punched in Celeste's number.

Even if it meant groveling, he would get Sage Medino back. It was a matter of pride.

Vivianne sat cross-legged on Sage's bed watching him toss clothes deftly into a suitcase. Now that Maya was gone he'd decided to return to L.A. and try to pick up the pieces of his life.

Although he was physically there, Vivianne already

missed him. She felt as if she were losing her best friend, and was torn between returning to Miami and completing the rest of her trip.

Why did she want to go home? She had no job and no immediate prospects in sight. Things seemed hopeless, and bad memories were bound to arise. But could she continue to travel without Sage, knowing that the men who were after her still hadn't been caught?

The police had called today with an update. The man taken into custody had admitted that he was hired by an American to scare Vivianne. It left her feeling uneasy. Those men could return at any time.

"Why do you have to rush back?" Vivianne asked, her eyes fastening on Sage's bare back and rippling muscles as he tossed shirts into his suitcase. Just looking at his half-naked body turned her on.

Sage shrugged. "I don't have to rush back, I suppose. But my job is done. I feel like I'm wasting time when I could be doing something else."

Vivianne sucked in a deep breath. Her eyes traveled the length of him, taking in the bronze hairs at the base of his neck and dusting his pectorals. Golden hairs disappeared beneath the open waistband of Sage's jeans. Dry-mouthed, she continued to stare. What seemed like minutes ago, his powerful hands had done the most incredible things to her. He'd held her, crushing her up against him. They'd sweated together and she'd felt the graze of those hairs against her breasts, igniting a fire in her that she didn't know she possessed.

Vivianne tried one last time. "We don't necessarily have to catch up with the group," she said. "I know we've prepaid for lodging, food, and entertainment, but why can't we simply stay here and take in the sights like normal tourists?"

Sage stopped what he was doing and came to sit beside her. One hand cupped her chin, tilting it back. "You have no idea how much I'm tempted."

"I would love it if you stayed here with me," she said. "I enjoy your company."

"I'm very tempted," Sage said, touching his lips to her temple and driving her wild. His fingers drew rings around the nape of her neck. He slid the straps of her camisole down her arms and her breasts were exposed. A whisper of a breeze blew through the open window making her nipples even tauter. Sage suckled on one and manipulated the other.

"What do I have to do to convince you to stay with me?" Vivianne asked, her hands trailing down his back.

"If you continue doing what you're doing, I just might say yes."

She slid her hands into his open jeans and found his hot spot.

"Oh, yeah. I like that a lot," Sage said.

"Well, what will it be?" Vivianne asked, her hands finding his scrotum and squeezing gently.

Sage groaned. "How is a man expected to think clearly when you're doing that?" He shifted his weight, his arm muscles bulging.

"Just say yes. I would be interested to see if Sage Medina, ex-FBI agent, allows me to get inside his head."

Sage blew a hot breath against her temple. "You're in my head, baby. You're in my head."

His admission made her realize she was playing with fire. She'd known Sage liked her and found her attractive. Their lovemaking since that night had taken a different turn. It had become tender and more giving. But she would never have guessed that she'd gotten inside his head. What she wanted more was to get under his skin and put her brand on him.

Sage found a condom in his wallet, palmed it, and settled on top of Vivianne. He reached into his pants and freed his erection and shielded himself. She slid her bikini briefs aside and he entered her quickly. Together they found a comfortable rhythm.

As the pace picked up, Vivianne felt herself go flush. Sage rolled her onto her side, both hands claiming her breasts. She could feel every inch of him, smell his raw sexuality and hear his uneven breathing. When he slammed into her, she cried out. In concert, they exploded.

Reality returned when the phone rang, shattering their euphoria.

"Damn, talk about bad timing," Sage groused. "I'm tempted not to answer it."

"Then don't."

Since Maya was no longer an issue, he wasn't inclined to jump when a phone rang. He seemed more relaxed, looser, and a lot more spontaneous.

The phone continued to ring. Sighing, Sage rolled off Vivianne. He picked up the receiver and barked into it. "Hello."

A look of astonishment transformed his face as he held the receiver away from his ear and mouthed, "It's Errol."

Vivianne poked him in the side. "Who's Errol?"

Sage covered the mouthpiece and turned back to her. "Errol's my ex-boss."

Vivianne sat up, listening intently to the one-sided conversation.

"Why are you calling me?" She heard Sage say. He had a viselike grip on the receiver and his jaw muscles twitched. Vivianne was afraid it would explode in his hand.

"So I'm just supposed to say that I'm ready to come back to work. I'm to accept your apology just like that," he said.

Vivianne poked him again. "You're being offered your job back. Oh, Sage, how wonderful," she whispered.

He continued speaking. "How much back pay are we talking about?" His raised eyebrows indicated that the figure was astronomical.

"That's quite a bit of dough. I'll be on the next plane to discuss this in person."

After hanging up, he stretched out on the bed, draping an arm over his forehead.

"Aren't you going to fill me in?" Vivianne asked after several minutes elapsed.

Sage heaved a huge sigh and rolled onto his side, facing her. "The bureau admits they've made a mistake. I've been totally cleared of all charges. Another agent was caught red-handed and under duress, confessed to stealing the drugs. They're offering me my job back, complete with back pay."

"How do you feel about that? You should be ecstatic," Vivianne said, ignoring the pain in her gut, and the deep sadness that had surfaced. Sage had just told her he was heading home.

"I'm numb," Sage admitted. "I'm not sure how I should feel."

Determined to make the few hours that were left memorable, Vivianne laid her head on his chest. Her fingers stroked his washboard stomach and trailed downward. She wouldn't think about his leaving. She would live for the moment and enjoy what little time they had left.

"Make love to me," Vivianne said, hugging him. "Make me forget that you'll soon be gone."

Sage wrapped his arms around her and pulled her close. "With pleasure. You're one woman I will never forget."

She knew she would never forget him either. But she couldn't tell him that. It all seemed so hopeless.

Fourteen

Alec had raced through the airport, hoping to find Maya, determined to make her listen to his explanations. It was important that she understand why he'd done what he'd done.

By the time he'd checked out the monitors and figured out Maya's gate, her plane was already taxiing down the runway. Feeling like a chump, he managed to make his own flight by the skin of his teeth.

Six days later, he was back in New York. Despite jet lag and the grime accumulated from almost a day's travel, it felt good to be home. Alec had caught up with the tour group in Athens, and even gone sight-seeing with the herd. Touring the Parthenon had been a dream, and he'd spent every free moment sketching. That action had kept him occupied and focused.

They'd gone on to Germany where Alec consumed more than his fair share of beer. He'd eaten a sausage or two, and taken his life into his hands driving at high speed on the Autobahn. Yet something was still missing.

At night, when he had time to think, he acknowledged the missing part of him was Maya; still he refused to admit that he was hurting. Alec Randolf didn't hurt. Hurting was for sissies, men who couldn't handle their emotions.

Damn, but he did miss Maya. He missed her ready smile and her go-with-the-flow attitude. They'd had a good time together. He regretted that he hadn't pursued her more ardently.

He never should have allowed her to walk away. It made good sense to put the whole thing behind him and move on. There would be other women, women who lived in the same town as he. Females who shared his background.

After clearing customs, Alec followed the signs for public transportation. He was down to his last twenty dollars and a taxi was not an option. Outside, he inhaled the familiar smell of gasoline fumes and listened to the racket of a million voices as passengers negotiated a means to get home.

Two hours later, he hopped off the bus in Brooklyn and trudged down his mother's street. Flatbush was experiencing an early summer, and the gardens in front of the brownstones were filled with wilting tulips and dying daffodils.

"Hey, boy. Haven't seen you in a while," one of his mother's neighbors called in greeting.

"I've been out of town. Catch you later."

Alec mounted the steps of the four-story building and headed for the apartment his mother rented. No need to knock, he had his own key. His mother wouldn't be home anyway, but he couldn't wait to see his sister, Trina.

Just as he expected, his teenage sister was seated at the kitchen table doing her homework. She looked up, greeted him with a squeal, and sent the chair behind her flying.

"Alec," she yelled, "I didn't expect you." She threw herself into his arms, beaded braids swirling around her.

"Hey, short stuff, easy. You're getting too heavy for me to pick you up."

"Short stuff" was a running joke between them. Trina was reed-thin and close to six feet, a couple inches shorter than he.

"So what did you bring me?" Trina asked, toeing the bulging backpack he'd thrown on the floor.

"Me," Alec responded, giving her a wink. "Aren't I good enough?"

She folded her arms, light eyes—the same color as his—narrowing.

Alec removed a small sack from the pocket of his jean jacket and dangled it in front of her. Trina grabbed it from his hand, pulled the string open, and poured the contents into her hands. A kaleidoscope of colors spilled into her palms, colorful beads of every shape and size, some hitting the linoleum floor with a ping and rolling into the crevices.

Trina scrambled after them, scooping them up. "These are da bomb," she said. "You always did have good taste. When I get my hair braided again, I'll be sure to put them in. Now what else did you bring me?"

"Who said I brought you anything else?" Alec teased. "When's Mom getting home? What's for dinner?"

Trina pouted and pointed to the stove. "Mom won't be home until the weekend. She's got this new job in Jersey. Mrs. Bailey down the street looks in on me."

Alec's eyes narrowed. He hated the thought of Trina being left alone. "Mom didn't tell me she'd changed jobs," he said.

"How would you know if you didn't call?" Trina reprimanded him.

To hide his embarrassment and annoyance at himself, Alec crossed over to the stove and lifted the lids on the pots. Things must have been pretty bad for his mother to leave Trina unsupervised. She was a responsible teenager but a teenager nevertheless.

His sister had fried chicken and heated up Sunday's leftover ribs. There were mashed potatoes and green beans, food for the soul. It had been a long time since he'd had a meal like this. He heaped portions onto his plate and sat.

"This came for you," Trina said as he was digging in. She set an official-looking envelope on the Formica table and took the seat across from him.

Alec squinted at the return address. It was from some guy with a title, Adam Rubenstein, Esq. What could an attorney want with him? Not unless Maya . . . No, she wouldn't. Couldn't. He ripped open the envelope and read the letter.

"I'll be damned." Still trying to absorb the information, he tossed the letter down.

"Watch your mouth," Trina said. "You know Ma doesn't like you to curse."

The address listed was Park Avenue. Pretty swanky and high-priced. The attorney wanted Alec to call him.

"Something the matter?" Trina asked. "Looks like you're tripping big time."

"Not tripping, just confused. This lawyer wants to talk to me."

"What about?" Trina nibbled on the end of her pencil, her mind on her homework again. "Tell me you're not in trouble, Alec?"

"Not that I know of."

It was after six, and too late to call Adam Rubenstein. Alec concentrated on his meal, wolfing down chicken and stuffing mashed potatoes into his mouth. He'd planned on having dinner, visiting with his mother, then returning to the apartment he shared in East Harlem with three other students. Now that he'd found out Trina was alone, plans changed. He'd stay until the weekend when his mother got home.

Tomorrow he would call Rubenstein. Meanwhile, keeping an eye on Trina would give him something to do, and take his mind off Maya.

"What exactly are you saying?" Kathryn Samuels asked, giving the man in front of her a skeptical look. He'd just repeated the most preposterous story she'd ever heard.

"You can verify that what I'm saying is true if you just listen to the tape," Todd Aikens responded, slamming a small rectangular object on her desk. Kathryn saw it was a tape recorder.

She sat back in her chair, a finger twirling the delicate pearl of her earring.

"You're saying that Vivianne Baxter was set up? That she never sexually harassed Harold Huggins, or any man that you're aware of? Why, Todd, haven't you come forward before?"

Todd twitched visibly. Kathryn gave him a steely-eyed look. "Because Harold was my manager and I was afraid to speak up."

"Harold still manages you; in fact, he's in a higher position."

Kathryn hadn't had much interaction with Todd Aikens, except for when he'd come forward to support Harold's accusations of sexual harassment. For the most part the clerk kept to himself, which was why his testimony was so credible. He seemed to have no ax to grind, but she had to be sure.

Under her intense scrutiny, Todd appeared to shrink. Kathryn became relentless, determined to get to the bottom of this. She'd always had immense respect for Vivianne, and had been her mentor. Letting her protégée go had hurt her deeply.

"If this story is true," Kathryn said, "how could you allow a respected member of management to be wrongfully dismissed? How were you able to live with yourself?"

Todd shifted uneasily, refusing to meet her eyes.

"What was I to do?" he said. "I was between a rock and a hard place. My loyalty to Harold won out. When he came to me and said he needed a witness, I repeated what I believed to be true. Just listen to the tape and draw your own conclusions."

"Where is your loyalty now?" Kathryn asked shrewdly. "Something must have happened to make you change your mind. Aren't things working out in your office?"

Todd hung his head. "It's not that. I've felt guilty ever since.

Harold has always wanted Vivianne's job, he hated being managed by a woman. When I confronted him, he admitted that he'd come up with a scheme to get rid of Vivianne. I was upset. I talked to my wife. She convinced me to talk to you. She said I'd never be able to forgive myself if I didn't."

"Suppose I call Harold in? Are you prepared to repeat what you just told me?" Kathryn asked.

"If I have to," Todd said. "Listen to the tape." He tapped the tape recorder that lay between them.

Kathryn gave Todd another calculated stare. She couldn't help being suspicious. Something just didn't seem right.

"You mentioned that Harold hired men to scare Vivianne; why would he do that if he's gotten what he wanted? She no longer works here and shouldn't pose a threat."

"Harold thought Vivianne knew too much. He and a buddy were stealing from the company. Vivianne walked in on a conversation and heard him talking about some missing checks. He's afraid that now the heat's off, she might go to the media with her story. He's scared to go to jail. You should audit the books."

"This is a very serious accusation," Kathryn said, standing and peering at him over the rims of her half-moon glasses.

The accounts had been quickly reviewed when Vivianne had brought up the subject. There'd been no entries in the ledger to support her statement. It had been thought that she was trying to take the heat off of herself.

Kathryn's hands closed around the recorder. She would listen to the tape later and then decide how to proceed. She'd never cared for Harold Huggins, but his work had been exemplary, making him the obvious choice when Vivianne's position came open.

Kathryn slipped the recorder into her briefcase. "I'll get back to you, Todd. Please see yourself out."

* * *

Vivianne picked up the receiver, then put it down for what seemed the hundredth time. Ever since returning to Miami, she'd wanted to call Sage and see how he was doing. But something stopped her. Let Sage call her. Let him make the first move.

She paced the length of her tiny Coral Gables home that had been no more than a cottage when she first bought it. Wandering through the rooms, Vivianne reverently touched the old furniture she'd painstakingly refinished. She was proud of the house, proud that she'd turned a handyman special into a home. She'd bought it before prices in that area went crazy, using up the money her grandmother had left her for a down payment. It had been money well spent. The Coral Gables address alone would assure a tidy profit.

Vivianne had sunk every disposable dime into the house, doing some of the renovations herself, relying on friends, or the boyfriends of the women she'd assisted, to help with the more complicated stuff like plumbing and wiring. Just thinking about it made her miss the work she enjoyed so much.

She'd returned to Miami on the same day Sage left for Los Angeles. They'd said a mercifully brief good-bye. Sage had thought it best she go home. So she'd given the police her number in the States and gotten on a plane, heartbroken. Now it had been two whole days, and she still hadn't heard from him.

"Damn the man," she muttered to herself, heading for the tiny galley kitchen that overlooked an equally small courtyard. "Why did I have to hook up with him to begin with?"

At least the media was no longer camped on her doorstep, thank God. Vivianne Baxter was old news, and her comings and goings no longer mattered.

Vivianne took a seat on the wrought-iron stool she'd sanded and painted a canary yellow. The cushions she'd made herself, choosing a complementary fabric of red, yellow, and green. She poured a Cuban coffee, savoring the bittersweet liquid, and downed a mouthful.

The newspaper she'd picked up earlier sat unopened. She spread the pages wide and leafed through the classified ads. Her savings were rapidly being depleted and she couldn't sit idle forever. But who would hire her? No one wanted someone who'd been involved in a scandal. Maybe she should consider moving, but giving up her house and selling her possessions seemed a daunting task. Miami had been her home for twenty-odd years. She'd gone to high school and graduated from college here. She'd made nice friends, and was still close to the few that were left.

Concentrate, Vivianne. Concentrate on the ads. She found the professional section but nothing caught her interest. Nothing she wanted to do. She wasn't just looking for a job; she needed to feel worthwhile, to give something back to the community. It had to be a position with merit, something where she could help those less fortunate than she was.

Exhausting her options in the paper, she planned her next move. In a minute she would turn on her computer and start checking out sites like Monster.com or Jobs.com. They had to have something.

The phone rang and she leapt for it.

A throaty voice filled the earpiece. "Hola, mamita, I heard you were back. How come so soon?"

Vivianne's dark mood lightened. It was Lourdes Dominguez, her best friend. Loyal Lourdes, who'd believed in her innocence and who'd urged her to fight WOW tooth and nail.

"Hi, hon," Vivianne said. "I meant to call, but you know how that goes."

"How was your trip?" Lourdes asked.

"It served a purpose, helped me keep my mind off my troubles."

"Meet anyone interesting?"

It was inevitable, Lourdes was bound to ask. They'd always traded stories about their dates, chuckling about the strange men they encountered. Vivianne hesitated; should she tell Lourdes about Sage?

"Actually, I did," she said. "I met a man from California. But it's hopeless."

Lourdes's husky laughter made Vivianne laugh too. "You sure know how to pick them. California's a long ways away, baby. Come on, gimme the 411. I'm dying to hear."

Vivianne skipped the details. Her encounter with Sage had been a brief interlude. Lourdes didn't need to know he was different and special. She didn't need to know how much Vivianne missed him. Time to move on with her life, find a job and start living again.

A sharp beep punctuated the conversation. Call-waiting was inconvenient at times.

Vivianne sighed, her eyes rolling heavenward. "Hold on a sec, Lourdes," she said, "there's another call coming in." Punching a button, she greeted the caller. "Hello."

"Vivianne?"

The woman's voice was familiar but she couldn't quite place it.

"Yes, this is she."

"Kathryn Samuels, here."

Viviane felt herself begin to hyperventilate. She jumped up, taking the cordless receiver with her, and entered the living room.

"Vivianne?"

"I'm here."

She studied the olive-colored walls with their tropical border, and took several calming breaths. Kathryn was the last person she'd expected to hear from.

Despite her best efforts not to rehash the nightmare, it came back vividly now. She'd been let go from a five-year job. Kathryn, who had been her boss and mentor, had turned her back on her, believing everything that awful Harold Huggins had said.

"Vivianne?" Kathryn repeated. "Talk to me."

Talk about what? She'd experienced the deep pain of disappointment and the ache of betrayal. "Can you hold for a minute?" she asked. "I have someone else on the line. Don't hang up."

Vivianne got Lourdes back, explaining that Kathryn was on the phone.

"Oh, mamita, you call me back the minute you find out what she wants," Lourdes said, hanging up.

"I'm back," Vivianne said to Kathryn, and waited.

"I'm calling to offer you your old job back," Kathryn said without preamble.

"What?"

Vivianne felt as if she would faint, despite the cool air-conditioning. She crossed to the French doors, threw them open, and stepped out onto the patio, where huge terra-cotta pots of geraniums swayed in the breeze.

"What are you saying, Kathryn?"

Kathryn's polished tones became brisk and matter-of-fact. "We have confirmed that Harold Huggins made up an incredible story about you. We audited our books and found large sums of money missing, donations from major organizations. You were right all along. On behalf of WOW I offer you my most sincere apologies."

Did Kathryn expect her to feel elated? Grateful? She'd gone through hell. An apology wasn't enough.

"I don't know," Vivianne said.

"Harold has been fired and so were Bill and the young man, Todd Aikens, who came forward with the story. We hope that we're able to keep the news out of the *Herald*. Todd's tale was backed up by a taped admission. WOW admits it made a terrible mistake. We'd like to make it up to you. If you desire a public apology, then that's what we'll do."

Warm tears streamed down Vivianne's cheeks. She tilted her face toward the morning sun, hoping it would soothe her anger. The job she'd loved, lived for, was being offered back. Yet she could never forget the humiliation of being vilified, tarred and feathered—of being labeled a loose woman who couldn't keep her hands off men. How was she to speak publicly, and with any conviction, about an organization she no longer felt good about? How would she ever gain respect again?

She might need a job, but this was not it. When the news broke about misappropriated funds, WOW would have a hard time of it, just like the other not-for-profit organization that recently had been in that position. It would be years before WOW would regain the public's trust. Some might say she was crazy to walk away from a career that paid well and that others coveted, but she just couldn't go back.

"Well, what do you say?" Kathryn said. "WOW needs you, Vivianne. There's not a day that goes by that the women you've helped haven't called asking about you."

The lump in Vivianne's throat tightened and threatened to choke her. She'd missed those women, missed giving them a shot. She'd watched their confidence grow when they realized that with earning power they gained control of their lives.

She took a deep breath. "I'm going to have to say no."

"What?" Kathryn sounded as it she were strangling.

"I can't come back," Vivianne repeated. "It's too late."

"Have you found something else? We'll match the salary."

"I'm still looking."

"But what will you do?" Kathryn asked. "Miami only has so many professional jobs."

"I'll find something."

What Kathryn said was true. There was a limited professional pool in Miami, but there was always Broward County. And if necessary, much as it pained her, she'd sell her beautiful house. A change of venue might be just the thing.

"Sleep on my offer," Kathryn said.

Vivianne's mind was already made up. There was no going back.

Fifteen

"Hey, girl. Why are you out here alone?"

The light-skinned man, attractively attired, let his eyes roam over Maya. He held out the glass of champagne in his hand. "Have a sip."

"No, thank you," Maya answered, resenting the intrusion. "Did you follow me here?"

The man gave her a calculated grin and sipped from his glass. "Let's just say I spotted you and thought you were someone I'd like to get to know."

It was her friend Shelley's twenty-first birthday. Anyone who was anyone had been invited to the party. Maya had forced herself to mingle, exchanging the usual small talk and dancing with an assortment of shallow young men. All that forced gaiety had served to bring on a huge headache. Finally sick of it all, she'd wandered out here. The truth was, she missed Alec, and none of the men present even came close.

Maya had followed a sloping pathway and found the guest cottage. She'd flopped down on the steps, and grown increasingly more depressed. Life seemed empty now.

"Things couldn't be that bad," the stranger said, intruding on her thoughts. He flashed another dynamic smile, the corners of his eyes crinkling.

At another time, Maya would have found him handsome. She tried responding to his smile, though her heart just wasn't in it. He seemed pleasant enough, certainly different from the rest of the Hollywood jet set.

The party so far had been a showcase for excess and waste. Mounds of caviar had been served on silver platters. Champagne spilled from fountains, and a martini bar had been erected even though many of the invitees were underage. There was lobster and sushi, filet mignon and prime rib. For those perpetually on a diet, there was low-fat everything. No one cared that there were those in America still starving.

Maya's companion sat on the step below her, sipping his drink and eyeing her over the rim of his glass.

"What's your name?" he asked.

"Maya."

"Does Maya have a last name?"

She hesitated. Telling him would only produce the usual response. "Gabriel," she said, reluctantly.

He didn't blink, didn't seem to know who she was. He continued smoothly, "And beautiful Maya wants to be alone. Where have you been all my life? You haven't been at any of the parties."

That much was true. Ever since returning from Europe she hadn't been in the mood. If it wasn't for the fact that she liked Shelley she would not be here.

Maya noted her companion's expensive linen shirt. Armani, if she were to guess. The shirt was set off by elegant pants and a polished pair of Gucci's, minus socks. He obviously was no one's poor relative.

"What's your name?" she asked, since it seemed the polite thing to do.

"Brad Fox. I'm a friend of a friend of the birthday girl. I'm visiting from New York."

She mouthed the customary response. "Nice to meet you, Brad."

He settled in more comfortably, crossing one long leg

over the other. "And why is Maya sitting alone out here while her friends are in the main house partying?"

"I wasn't much in the mood," she admitted.

Brad studied her gravely and offered another sip of his drink. "Looks like you could use this."

"No, thanks. Alcohol would only make me more depressed than I am."

"It's ginger ale," he said, offering her the glass again. "Booze I never touch."

Curiosity got the better of her. He seemed smoother than smooth, comfortable with himself. Guys of Brad's type were usually drinking men.

Maya took a tentative sip of his drink.

"So how come you don't drink alcohol?" she asked. "You must be over twenty-one."

"I'm twenty-five. And I don't drink because the stuff makes me crazy."

Maya was surprised by his admission. "You're an alcoholic," she guessed.

Brad flashed her a winning Colgate smile. "I could be, easily, except I'm smart enough to know when to stop. Something tells me you have man problems."

A girl simply didn't unload on a man she just met. But she needed to talk to someone, and Brad seemed willing to listen.

"I'm getting over a relationship that went sour," Maya admitted.

"The man had no taste." Brad gave her a wink.

He seemed a nice enough guy, funny and genuinely interested in her. Too bad she wasn't interested in him.

"Oh, Alec had great taste," she said. "He was offbeat, nontraditional, and down-to-earth, qualities sadly lacking in these Hollywood types. But he turned out to be just another player."

"And you meet a lot of those?" Brad said, his lips twitching. His fingers circled her wrists. "Go on."

Maya chuckled. She was starting to feel a whole lot better. She told him the whole convoluted story, ending with "And I caught him stealing, imagine that."

When she was through, he said, "What if Alec was telling you the truth? What if you let him walk out of your life without really listening? Life's too short to let pride get in the way."

Pride, this wasn't about pride. This was about someone taking advantage of her. Someone she had grown close to, someone she had come to love. Someone she had slept with, who'd used her.

"Then how do you explain waiting until I fell asleep to go through my stuff? He was caught with my travelers checks in hand."

"How do you know he actually meant to steal those checks? Maybe he meant to ask you about them later."

Good point. But she'd been quick to judge. Quick to jump to conclusions.

Maya's shoulders sagged. Her previous bad mood was returning.

She shook her head. "It's hopeless. Alec's in New York and I'm here. After the way I behaved he's not going to want to talk to me."

Brad tilted her chin and looked into her eyes. "I doubt that, Maya. He'd be a fool."

Before she could figure out what he was doing, he kissed her. It was a quick peck, but one with promise. Had it not been for Alec, it was a kiss that would have been worth exploring.

"You've got it bad," Brad said, releasing her. "That felt like a brother kissing his sister. Go find your stud. Manhattan isn't that big a place."

He placed a hand in his pants pocket and pulled out a cell phone. "Call him. You won't be happy until this is resolved and I won't have a snowball's chance in hell of dating Maya Gabriel."

Alec's number burned a hole her purse. She'd taken the number out often and stared at it. Dare she call him?

"Punch in those numbers," Brad said, walking away. "If it doesn't go well I'll be at the main house. Please come to find me."

Maya held the phone in her hand. She thought for a moment and then began punching the numbers. There was nothing to lose except her pride. Why not give it a shot?

"It's good having you back," John Sylvester said, clinking his beer bottle against Sage's. "I missed you, bro." John took a long slug of his drink and scanned the bar, checking out the patrons.

"It's great being back. Nice to be doing something useful instead of shadowing some child."

"I thought you said the movie stars' daughter was pretty cool."

"That she was."

Sage grinned at his friend. They'd spent the last hour reminiscing and downing numerous beers. Neither was drunk.

The volume level in the bar had steadily risen. An after-hours crowd filtered in, spilling from the booths and hugging the walls. All seemed intent on slugging down brew and catching up on the gossip. Sage caught an acquaintance's eye and nodded an acknowledgement. Another veteran spotted him and sauntered over.

"Hey," the agent said, "what's this I hear about you being offered a director's position?"

"You heard wrong, Craig."

Sage played dumb, waiting for the man to go on. He'd been invited to interview, but nothing definite had been promised. He assessed Craig, wondering about his agenda. He could be making conversation or he might simply be curious. It paid to be wary in this business. In a dog-eat-dog world, a directorship was a coveted slot. Best to keep his mouth shut and his ears open.

"I heard the news from a reliable source," Craig persisted. "Three of you are being considered, but rumor has it the job is yours if you want it."

"And who would this reliable source be?" Sage asked, signaling to the waitress for another round.

"You know better than to ask me that." Craig slid into the booth and sat down. In conversational tones he continued, "You'd be nuts to turn down that primo job and all the dinero. Come on, spill it, don't play dumb."

Sage knew he would be nuts to turn it down, but nothing definite had been offered to him, at least not yet.

John, sensing Sage's discomfort, skillfully changed the subject. "Hey," he said to Craig, "let's hear about your new assignment."

Craig puffed his chest. "Someone's been flapping their gums. I get to hunt down the serial killer that has all those Brentwood babes scared."

"Working that upscale neighborhood is a tough assignment," said John.

"Here you go," their waitress interrupted, setting down drinks in front of them. The conversation went off in another direction.

"Check out Adrienne Rosario. God, she's one hot babe." Craig drooled. His eyes practically popped out of his head at the sight of Adrienne's shapely derriere.

Sage's gaze shifted to Adrienne though he wasn't in the least interested in her, or any of the females buzzing around the bar. His focus now was work. Anything to forget Vivianne. He'd logged in an enormous number of hours, hoping to take his mind off her. It was senseless to want a woman who lived on another coast. Nothing could come of it, so he hadn't called her.

"So what you been up to during this little vacation of

yours?" Craig asked, his eyes never leaving Adrienne's firm behind.

Sage shrugged. "I kept busy and managed to make money."

"Yeah, yeah. I heard you were playing bodyguard to some rich babe."

Sage eyed him suspiciously. "You seem to keep quite well informed."

"I make a point of it. Good to hear there's life after the FBI."

"Be assured there is."

A coffee-colored woman of average height sashayed by them. From the back she reminded Sage of Vivianne. Sensing them staring, she turned and smiled. Pretty as she was, Vivianne was prettier. Best to forget about her and concentrate on his job.

The television was on and a group of men huddled around watching the game. Sage, glad for an excuse, focused on it. A newscaster came on, interrupting the play. He droned on about muggings, mayhem, and national disasters. Sage briefly lost interest until a familiar face flashed on the screen. Vivianne had made the news again. Body wired, he focused in on the report.

In clipped tones, the newscaster said, "Vivianne Baxter has made headlines again. Baxter, the ex-spokesperson of WOW, was accused of sexually harassing a male employee. She was subsequently terminated and replaced by one of her alleged victims. Now, four months later, WOW has come forward to say they made a mistake. A public apology is being issued to Baxter and she's been offered her job back. We can only wonder why she has declined to accept. Harold Huggins, one of Ms. Baxter's accusers, is charged with defrauding the system and may spend a long time in prison."

"Go, Vivianne," Sage wanted to say out loud. Her version had been accurate, not that he'd doubted that for a minute.

He'd tried putting her out of his mind and now in the most unexpected way he'd been forced to think about her again. Vivianne had provided the balance he needed. He'd admired her tenacity and her determination not to be a victim. She'd been driven by conviction, but was in no way overbearing. He liked that she hadn't rolled over and died.

She easily could have. They'd met at a time when they were both down and out. Yet Vivianne had never once felt sorry for herself; he had to admire that. What would she be like now that she was back in the States, her name finally cleared? One phone call to see how she was doing wouldn't hurt. He owed her at least that.

Coming to that decision, Sage set down his beer bottle and prepared to take off. This noisy, smoky bar was not conducive to clear thought or concocting a plan. And he needed a plan if he were to see Vivianne again.

Sage said his good-byes quickly and exited.

Alec sat speechless, arms crossed over his chest, heart pounding. He still hadn't grasped what he'd just heard.

"Over two million dollars?" he repeated like a zombie.

"That's right, son."

The news of his inheritance left him numb. He should be jumping for joy, but this was hush money, and much as he needed it, he couldn't accept.

Adam Rubenstein, the attorney, sat behind a ridiculously small desk, pudgy fingers smudging the glass. He read slowly from the document, enunciating every last word. Louis Taylor, the father Alec had never known, had entrusted this man with his last will and testament.

"Your father was my client for over thirty years. I handled his legal issues from the day he opened his first antique shop. I was his adviser and friend. He trusted me. When his business became profitable he was forced to expand. One antique store turned into many and Louis made smart investments."

"How did he die?" Alec asked, not because he particularly cared, but because it was expected.

"From a heart attack. Louis has left his properties to his wife and children but to you he left this incredible sum. Two million dollars is a lot of money, and it's contingent on you opening up a business you enjoy."

He should be doing cartwheels, but the news still hadn't penetrated. It left Alec suspicious. What was the catch? Why had his father felt it necessary to acknowledge him after all of these years? As Adam continued to read, Alec's distrust slowly turned to shock. He could do quite a bit with a couple of million dollars; it would help win Maya back.

"Well, what do you say, Alec?" Adam asked, regarding him over his black-framed glasses. "Will you accept your inheritance?"

Alec's gaze shifted to regard the stuffy lawyer. He laughed derisively. "What took Louis all this time to acknowledge me? He never wanted me, never reached out to me when he was alive—now in death he hopes to make this right? What about my mother? What about her?"

"Louis cared about your mother. He cared about you," Adam said, unfolding his heavy frame from the chair and standing. "He tried to make contact with your mother on numerous occasions. He wrote to her and even tried calling to offer financial support. He wanted to be a part of your life but your mother ignored him. Her reasoning remains a mystery to me."

Alec refused to let the attorney see how upset he was. Did he think he'd fallen off a milk truck? The story Dominique told him while he was growing up was that he'd been abandoned, his existence ignored. Why would his mother go to such lengths to keep him away from his father?

"Something's not right," Alec said, giving the attorney a

piercing look. "Just like that, Louis Taylor leaves me a couple million dollars?"

"Your father has always acknowledged his paternity. His wife learned to live with that fact. Why your mother chose to exclude him from her life is something only she knows. My client did everything possible to contact her."

"Like hell he did," Alec said, standing and pounding his fist on the glass surface. "My mother's no liar."

"Calm down, son." Adam Rubenstein held his hands up. "I know you're angry. But it's not every day that someone inherits this kind of money. If you invest it well you'll be set for life."

"I don't want Louis Taylor's money," Alec burst out, even though the amount was finally sinking in. He could pay off his student loans, continue school, and pursue his dream of owning an art gallery. The money could buy canvases and paint, and set his mother and sister up for life.

"Your father wanted you to have an inheritance," Adam said gently. "He felt it was the least he could do."

Emotions too confusing to fathom roiled inside Alec. His anger continued to boil, finally exploding. "All these years my mother worked like a dog to put food on the table and a roof over our heads. She had no one. Now I'm supposed to accept money so some old man can go to heaven with a clear conscience."

"You're not thinking clearly," Adam said. "Your father has always wanted to do the right thing. He was willing to step up and shoulder responsibility. I have his letters to prove it. They were all returned to my office unopened."

Alec's mouth worked but nothing came out. Who was he supposed to believe, his hardworking mother or this emissary who had appeared out of nowhere? Two million dollars was more than he would ever earn in a lifetime. His mother and sister would be set. He could win Maya back. Alec tugged on the neck of his T-shirt, though the air conditioner continued to hum. He felt as if he might faint.

"Think it over," Adam said, rising from his chair and coming over to join him. "Sharon," he called to his secretary, "bring me Louis Taylor's entire file and bring in some water."

A strained silence descended. Alec's head buzzed. After a few minutes, Sharon, a brown-skinned honey, came tottering in, a bulging folder in one hand and the bottled water in the other.

"Here you are, Mr. Rubenstein," she said, turning the folder over and setting the water down on Adam's desk.

Alec's eyes focused on the file. It was so full that its contents spilled over the sides.

"Sit. Have a drink," Rubenstein said, pointing to the water.

Alec accepted the chilled bottle and with trembling hands uncapped it. Slowly he brought the bottle to his lips, sucking down the liquid in several quick swallows.

Adam Rubenstein dug through the folder and found what he was looking for. He slapped a stack of letters down in front of Alec. "Here, read for yourself."

Faced with confirmation of what Rubenstein had just told him, Alec's anger ebbed. His hands continued to shake as he picked up the bundled letters. There were dozens held together by a red rubber band. Alec held them for a moment, scared at what he might find. It wasn't easy confronting your past. His mother must have had her reasons for sending them back unopened, though it was difficult for him to understand why.

"They're stacked in chronological order," Adam said.

With trepidation, Alec removed the rubber band and reached for the last in the pile. He accepted the letter opener Adam handed him, but set it aside, preferring to use his numb fingers to rip open the envelope. Determined not to show any emotion, he pulled out two letters and began to read.

The first was from Adam Rubenstein.

Ms. Randolf:

My client, Louis Taylor, has asked me to contact you regarding a legal matter. A trust has been set up in the name of Alec Randolf, whom Louis Taylor acknowledges as his son. Please contact the law offices of Rubenstein and Rubenstein at the phone number listed below so that we can discuss the details of this trust.

Sincerely,
Adam Rubenstein, Esq.

The letter was dry and to the point. If his mother had followed up, they wouldn't be living as they currently were, hand to mouth, depending on his part-time job to supplement her housekeeping income. He extracted the second letter, sensing that it was of a more personal nature, and schooled his face to remain expressionless. Adam had resumed his seat.

My Dearest Dominique:

I trust this letter will make its way to you. I recently learned that you gave birth to my son. I am heartbroken that you did not contact me to tell me of his birth. We had a three-year relationship, one that I cherished, one that I prefer to think meant something to you. We were each other's best friends, we confided in each other and were lovers, yet you chose to bring a child into this world alone. I cannot fathom your reasoning. Surely you should know that even though I am married, I would never have turned my back on you.

I want to see my child. He is my flesh and blood. I

can only imagine that he is beautiful. I want to touch his ebony skin, play with his toes, and hear him giggle as I hold him close. I want to offer my financial and emotional support. I am in a comfortable position, and the least I can do is ensure that our child is cared for and educated. I do not know what I did to warrant your silence.

Enclosed is my check. I trust you will use the money to get yourself a nice apartment and buy the baby food and clothes. I will be sending you money on a monthly basis. What I would really like is for you to call me. I miss the sound of your voice and the warmth of your body next to mine. I miss the closeness we shared.

I will love you forever.

Your ever faithful,
Louis

Despite his resolve, Alec's eyes misted over. He felt as if he'd invaded someone's privacy. The last thing he'd expected was Louis's declaration of love. His mother had always painted a picture of his father as an uncaring man, one who'd abandoned her in a time of need. Yet the letter was written by a man obviously hurting.

Alec opened another letter and continued to read. It was filled with much of the same thing, pleas for his mother to make contact. Louis had been willing to take full responsibility for his child. Unable to continue, Alec pushed the pile across the desk and sat back.

Adam Rubenstein's kind eyes regarded him. "So what do you think?" He shoved his spectacles onto his head. "After reading those letters do you believe that your father willingly shirked his responsibilities?"

Alec stared at the attorney, his brain processing the information. Clearly his father had loved his mother. Even so, loyalty to his mother kicked in.

"If Louis felt this benevolent, why didn't he present himself at our door? My mother's address didn't change. She's lived there for twenty-plus years."

Adam steepled his fingers. "Maybe he feared rejection. Your mother was an independent soul. She returned his letters unopened, indicating she wanted nothing to do with him. Maybe Dominique didn't want to be responsible for breaking up his family. And when Louis found out that she married, he didn't want to complicate her life. The letters stopped."

Adam shoved documents and a pen Alec's way. "You'll need to sign these indicating you accept your inheritance."

Alec held the pen in his hand before placing it on the desk between them. "I'll get back to you. I want to talk to my mother and hear her side of the story." He pocketed the letters and rose.

"I'll wait for your call," Adam said, signaling his secretary. "Sharon, Mr. Randolf is about to leave, please show him out."

With a lot of hip-wiggling, Sharon appeared at Alec's side. "So what are you going to do with all that money?" she said, jiggling.

Alec shrugged, mumbling something he hoped she had the good sense not to ask him to translate.

"I'd go out and celebrate," Sharon said, her demeanor indicating she was angling for an invitation.

"Sharon," Rubenstein reminded her, "Mr. Randolf is leaving."

Alec followed the secretary out. Never in his wildest dreams had he thought he would be worth millions. His inheritance had come from a most surprising source.

Sixteen

Vivianne felt as if she had exhausted all of her options. What's more, her feet hurt. Really hurt. After updating her résumé, she'd followed every possible lead, and she had the blisters to prove it.

Vivianne had called every contact she knew in both Dade and Broward Counties. Finally she'd resorted to using headhunters. No one seemed interested in hiring her, leaving her to conclude that the negative press resulting from the scandal had labeled her off-limits.

She sat on Lourdes Domingues's small patio with her feet up, sipping wine and nibbling chips.

"Have you tried The United Way?" Lourdes asked, her feet propped up on a nearby table.

"I did. I interviewed for a position in fund-raising, but so far I've heard nothing."

"What about Jackson Memorial and other major hospitals? You'd be good in patient advocacy."

"I thought about that, but there's no money there. I have a mortgage and bills to pay. I need to cover my obligations."

Vivianne closed her eyes and took a deep breath, inhaling the scent of Lourdes's beautifully tended roses.

"You can't have everything, mamita," Lourdes said, regarding her through eyelashes thick with mascara. She sipped her drink. "Have you tried Habitat for Humanity?"

Vivianne shrugged. "They pay nothing."

"Then try a corporation."

There were few in Miami that Vivianne wanted to work for. The hopelessness of her situation plunged her into a deep funk. A cool breeze ruffled the rose bushes in Lourdes's tiny garden, and the perfumed scent wafting Vivianne's way did nothing to make her feel better. Dusk had descended, bringing with it little comfort.

"How's your cash holding up?" Lourdes asked, nibbling on a chip. "I could loan you money, if you like."

Things were getting tight but she wasn't at the point of having to borrow money from a friend.

"Thanks, but I don't need your money, at least not yet. Come fall, if I still don't have a job I'll tap into my money market."

"Not a good move. Are you still thinking about relocating?"

"I've considered it."

"And where will you go?" Lourdes asked, dribbling the last of the wine into their glasses and crossing one tanned leg over the other.

"I've thought about the Northeast, but I don't know if I can handle the winters."

"What about the Pacific Northwest?"

"Seattle or Oregon, hmmm . . . that's a thought."

"There's always the West Coast," Lourdes said, winking.

Vivianne shot Lourdes a look that could freeze water. The West Coast brought with it painful memories of Sage. He still hadn't called, and she'd been reluctant to make the first move.

Vivianne's cell phone rang. She was tempted to ignore it, but what if it was a potential employer?

"Are you going to get that?" Lourdes asked, jutting her jaw at the ringing phone.

Vivianne picked up before it clicked into voice mail. "Vivianne Baxter here."

"And how is Vivianne Baxter?" a deep male voice asked.

Her heart almost stopped. She forgot about Lourdes, who

she knew must be listening intently. She forgot about the low hum of cars as they zipped down the street. She struggled to breathe, forgetting how weary she was. She'd almost given up on Sage, and now he had called.

"Vivianne, are you there?"

She took a deep breath. "Yes, I'm here."

"How are you?"

"Fine. Holding my own."

"Have you found a job yet?"

Vivianne covered the mouthpiece. "It's the man I met in Venice."

"Oh," Lourdes said, sliding off her seat and walking toward the far side of the patio, pretending to study her potted plants.

"I'm still looking," Vivianne admitted. "How are you doing?"

"I'm back on the job. I have an assignment in Miami next week. I'll be in on Tuesday, will you be around?"

Oh, God, he was flying into Miami just as she was finally coming to grips with not having him in her life. *Breathe, Vivianne, hold on to your sanity.*

"Yes, I'll be around."

"Good. We'll plan on having dinner. Pick a nice place on South Beach."

"Have you heard from Maya?" Vivianne asked, changing the subject.

Sage didn't answer right off. "No. I haven't. I wanted to wait awhile before calling. Lest you forget, she was pretty angry with me."

"And me. But I wouldn't mind contacting her to see how she's doing."

"I'll give you her number, then."

He read Maya's phone number and Vivianne scrambled to find a pen and pad in her purse. She scribbled down the number.

"Give me your address," Sage demanded.

"What for?"

Lourdes, overhearing her tone, shot her a look of surprise and waggled a finger at her.

"So I can pick you up at you home," Sage said. "How does seven sound?"

"I'll be ready."

It could be seven, eight, or nine. It wasn't as if she had anything else to do.

"Seven it is, then."

"I've missed you, Vivianne."

She'd missed him too, but never in her wildest dreams had she expected Sage to admit it. Just hearing his husky voice made her wish that he was there, holding her, loving her.

"The feeling is mutual," she said, stiffly. What she really wanted to blurt out was that in the wee hours of the night, she lay wide awake thinking about him.

"Till Tuesday, then."

"Till Tuesday."

Life suddenly looked brighter and more hopeful. She disconnected the call and sat thinking.

Lourdes's voice intruded. "Spill it, *mamita.* I'm dying to hear."

Vivianne looked up into her friend's eager face. "Sage is coming to Miami on Tuesday. We're having dinner," she said.

Lourdes's laughter rang out. "At last I get to meet the man. I'll be at your house when he stops by."

No point in discouraging her. Lourdes would provide emotional support when Vivianne's legs turned to rubber. She was a good friend.

Alec stood in the drab kitchen, his hands on his hips.

"What gave you the right to keep this from me?" he demanded. He shook a crumpled piece of paper at his mother.

Dominique took a step back. She'd never seen her son this angry. She'd taken the train from New Jersey, not expecting to find Alec here.

As he advanced, she retreated. Alec waved the creased piece of paper at her.

"I met with an attorney earlier this week. Adam Rubenstein ring a bell with you?" One eyebrow, so like his father's, curved upward.

Devilishly handsome, just like his dad, Dominique thought, her stomach clenching. The fact that Alec mentioned Goldstein indicated he knew about his father. The past was rapidly closing in.

Louis Taylor had been the love of her life, although he'd never known it. He'd been married when Dominique went to work for his wife. It hadn't taken her long to figure out that the marriage was in name only. The couple shared little in common, not even a bedroom. They were staying together for the sake of their children.

Dominique had cleaned house and taken care of the couple's two sad kids, who were painfully aware that their parents were putting one foot in front of the other. At first, Louis had wanted someone to talk to, and talk he did. Their conversations had taken place late at night, when wife and children were safely in bed. Dominique had been amazed that as successful as Louis was, he worried incessantly about his business and his failure to connect with his wife.

Late night chats had turned into more intimate conversation. And during one of their more vulnerable moments, they'd ended up in bed. Dominique had chastised herself for letting it happen. But when it happened again, she realized that he was starving for company. She was offering him something his wife never could, unjudgmental listening and emotional support.

Dominique faced Alec. "How come you met with Adam Rubenstein?"

Her son regarded her stonily. "Because he contacted me. Here's the letter to prove it."

The paper he waved at her seemed official and frightening. She'd worked hard to forget about Louis, knowing they had no future together, knowing he would never leave his wife. When she'd become pregnant, she'd walked away, ignoring the letters and calls from his attorney.

"My father is dead," Alec said. "Did you know that?"

The loss of a man Dominique never really had, hit her full force. Pain ebbed and flowed through her. It had been years since she'd seen Louis, but her memories of him were still clear, comforting her at night when the hopelessness of her situation threatened to overwhelm her. While men had come and men had gone, including a husband, she'd never stopped loving Louis.

"Wh-what did Rubenstein want?" Dominique stuttered.

"He wanted to tell me about my inheritance."

"Louis left you money?" She gripped the kitchen chair while the kitchen walls folded like an accordion.

Alec's eyes never left her face. "Yes, he did. A huge sum. Over two million dollars."

The enormity of the amount sent her senses reeling, that, and the fact that Louis was no longer around.

"How did he die?" Dominique asked, struggling to breathe.

"Of a heart attack."

She sank into the chair. "Where's Trina?" She'd almost forgotten about her daughter.

"Out at the movies with a friend."

Alec hovered, still holding the damning letter. "Why did you keep my father's identity from me?"

"Because your father was not free to marry me."

Although Alec's jaw worked, nothing came out. Dominique wondered how she could explain her involvement with a married man. How could she tell Alec that she'd been thinking about him, them? That she'd hoped to save him pain?

"And you came to the conclusion I didn't need a father," Alec said. "I had to read Louis's letters to discover he wasn't the irresponsible, uncaring man you painted him to be. You cut him out of our lives without considering me."

"We didn't need him," Dominique said, truly believing that.

Alec's eyes flashed. He hung on to his composure by a thread. When he was able to talk, he said, "What are you, God? You had no right to decide I didn't need my father. I don't even know what the man looked like."

Dominique realized she'd made a mess of things. The son she loved more than life itself hated her. Desperate to make him understand, she pleaded, "Please listen to my side of the story."

"I'm listening," he said without a trace of a smile.

Difficult as it was, she charged ahead.

"I was young and impressionable when I first met Louis. He was an older man whom I admired. He was established, worldly, and paid attention to me. When I became pregnant I didn't want him to feel trapped. I knew his wife. I'd helped raise his kids; I didn't want to break up his marriage. It was easier to walk away, and a lot less complicated."

"Easier for who?" Alec said, circling the kitchen. "Do you know what it's like to grow up without a father? Do you know what it's like to have kids torment you and call you a bastard, to fill out a form and list your father as unknown? Damn it, Mama, why did you do that to me?"

Tears streamed down Dominique's cheeks in buckets. Alec had not called her Mama since he was an infant. Thankfully, Trina was not there to see her in this state. For the first time in years she doubted her decision.

"Where did Louis get that kind of money?" Dominique asked when she was able to pull herself together.

"He was quite prosperous and he invested well. His properties were left to his wife and kids, along with a sizable inheritance. Two million dollars was left to me."

It was slowly sinking in. Alec had inherited money.

"What will you do with all that cash?" Dominique asked.

Alec's hands cupped his head. He rocked on his heels. "I don't know, Mama. There's so much I could do. You won't ever have to clean houses again, or take care of someone's snotty kids. I'll buy you and Trina a home. I'll set up an art gallery. I'll . . . have my own home."

Tears started afresh down Dominique's cheeks. Angry as her son was, he was still thinking of them.

"Alec, would you really do that for us?" she asked.

"Sure. Annoyed as I am, I still love you and Trina."

Dominique opened her arms, hoping that Alec would come to her. He turned away and headed for the door. The cell phone in his pocket jingled and he stopped to glance at the number.

"Alec?" Dominique cried. "Alec, please don't leave." *Please, God, make him stop.*

Slowly he turned, tossing her the same tawny look as his father's. "I love you, Mother, but what you've done is hard to forgive."

"Alec," she pleaded again, "all I have are you and Trina."

"Us and your stupid pride," Alec said, slamming the door firmly behind him.

Seventeen

Maya depressed the button, disconnecting the call. She'd left at least a half dozen messages but Alec hadn't called back. All she'd gotten was that horrible answering machine of his.

Maya contemplated booting up her computer and sending him an e-mail. She didn't plan on letting him off that easily. At the very least, he would have to indicate he wanted nothing to do with her. Clutching the remote phone, she paced the spacious bedroom, debating the pros and cons of continuing to reach out to him.

After a while she tossed the receiver onto the bed and with a grim expression circled the room again. The bedroom was her haven, her expression of style. She'd decorated the room herself, despite her mother's efforts to have it professionally done. Maya didn't want a room so polished and perfect that she couldn't relax in it. She wanted it to reflect her personality and not some decorator's. The space should define who she was.

Disgusted with her negative thoughts, she plopped down on the divan she'd bought at an outdoor market, wrinkling the silk shawl that hid the worn spots in the process. She'd steadfastly refused to have it reupholstered. The divan suited her better than the elaborate sleigh bed, her one concession to her mother. The huge bed was filled with pillows, none of which matched. Across from the divan stood an oak armoire that held her collection of ebony-skinned dolls. Ten pairs of condemning brown eyes stared at her.

"Don't give me that look, Abigail," she said, glaring at one of the teak-colored dolls with its smug painted expression. "The man hates me. He won't even call back."

Abigail's answer never came. A soft tapping interrupted anything she was about to say.

Maya rolled her eyes and huffed out a breath. "Mother, is that you again?"

"It is, my dear."

"Fine. Come in, if you insist."

Maya knew it was futile to pretend she wasn't there. Nona had kept a careful eye on her ever since her return. Maya prepared herself for the unrelenting questions that had become the daily routine. Why couldn't her mother just leave her be?

The doorknob turned and Nona sailed in, high heels clicking across the wooden floors. She was between movies, and had time on her hands, time she chose to spend at home, time she spent interrogating Maya.

Her mother's expensive perfume drowned out the scent of the vanilla candles Maya had lit.

"I worry about you," Nona said, taking Maya's chin between her elegant hands, and forcing her daughter to look into her eyes. "You're too sad, baby. Talk to me."

Was it so obvious she was hurting? Once she'd loved the expensive baubles, liked the rambling old mansion that was her home, enjoyed the endless parties and plentiful food. All she had to do was ask, and it was hers. But now the glamorous, wasteful life of a Hollywood child no longer fulfilled her and she couldn't wait for school to resume. Not that she'd ever fit in to the scene.

"There's nothing to talk about," she said, shrugging out of her mother's grip.

Nona narrowed her eyes and pursed her perfectly shaped

lips. "You're not fooling me, darling. Something happened to you in Europe. You've changed since you got back."

Have not. Damn you, Abigail, stop looking at me.

Nona was relentless. "There's this young man, Brad Fox, who keeps calling. He sounds nice enough. Why don't you go out with him? Keep yourself busy."

Brad, nice as he was, was not the answer. After Alec, he seemed tame and unchallenging.

"Because I don't want to," Maya said.

Nona flicked imaginary dust off the silk shawl before angling onto the divan. She crossed one shapely leg over the other and raised an arched eyebrow. "I'm not moving from here until you talk to me."

"You'll be waiting a long time then," Maya said, picking up the remote and clicking on the television. Determined to shut her mother out, she stared at a rerun.

Nona's voice droned above the scripted dialogue. Maya wanted to yell at her and make her shut up.

"You've been listless and unhappy for some time. I have a good mind not to pay that useless Sage Medino until he tells me what's going on."

Maya rolled her eyes. "Gawd, Mother, you'd stoop so low as to not pay the man his salary because he wouldn't break a confidence? No wonder I couldn't wait to get away from you."

Nona placed a hand on her heart, feigning hurt. "A mother has to do what a mother has to do."

"You're despicable."

"And you're hurt. My primary concern is you."

Maya threw her hands in the air. Her mother showed no signs of leaving. If anything, she'd made herself more comfortable.

"Do you have a nail file, darling?" Nona asked, staring at one perfectly polished nail.

"No, I don't. I'm sure you have several in your room," Maya said pointedly. She jabbed the button of her computer, plopped down in the desk chair, dialed AOL, and waited for the connection to be made.

"You have mail," the mechanical voice chirped.

Maybe, just maybe, one of those messages was from Alec. Maya scrolled down the list of messages, deleting the junk. Several friends had checked in, asking how she was. Maya responded to some and ignored others. The rest could wait.

Her mother's voice intruded. "I'm not planning on going away, honey. If it takes all night I'll sit right here."

"Suit yourself," Maya snapped, shooting Nona another annoyed look, one her mother chose to ignore.

She turned her attention back to the screen. An instant message popped up from *Boywonder,* should she accept? Curiosity finally got the better of her. Maya clicked the word *Accept.*

Just got your messages, was gonna call you, Boywonder wrote.

Maya's heart practically stopped. Her mind shut down and her emotions took over. Her fingers froze on the mouse. Seconds ticked by. How to answer Alec?

Maya, are you there?

In body only—otherwise she was floating. It had been five long days since her first call. Five days of agonizing about Alec and thinking about him constantly. She'd thought about his beautiful body and all that dusky skin glistening with sweat. She'd thought about his labored breathing as he'd moved inside her, his slender artistic fingers strumming her body and bringing it to life. She missed him so much it hurt.

The anger had long since left her. It had been only money after all, a few crummy thousand that she could easily afford. And what if Brad was right? What if she'd made a terrible mistake and accused Alec falsely?

Another message filled the screen.

Maya, you aren't going to believe what's happened to me. I'm still tripping.

What happened to you? her stiff fingers typed.

Sign off and I'll call you.

Maya quickly severed the connection. She raced toward the bed and picked up the receiver from where she'd flung it. In just those few minutes of contact, her mood had lifted.

Nona, sensing the mood change, asked, "What's going on?"

Maya didn't answer immediately; her eyes remained on the phone, willing it to ring.

"Nothing's going on," she mumbled.

"Nothing put a sparkle back into your eyes, and a dance in your step?" her mother said, a smile curving her perfect lips. She unfurled her long, toned body from the divan, and went to stand next to her daughter.

The phone rang. Maya answered in an instant.

"Hello."

"Hey," Alec said. "Took you long enough to reach out to me."

She couldn't catch her breath. Couldn't find a quick comeback. Boy, had she missed him!

"Maya?" Alec's voice wavered.

"I'm here."

"Tell me you're no longer pissed at me."

She stood for a moment, holding the phone and trying to breathe. Covering the mouthpiece, she said to her mother, "Can I have my space?"

Nona's beautiful eyes narrowed. "There's a man on the phone. I knew it."

"Who's that?" Alec asked.

"Nobody."

Sniffing, Nona exited, muttering, "Nobody."

Just to be sure she'd left for good, Maya waited for the door to click shut.

"No. I'm no longer pissed at you," she answered. "But you've got a lot of explaining to do."

Alec's story sounded a lot more plausible now that she'd had time to simmer down.

"If I was looking to rob you," he said, "I would have snatched cash, not travelers checks."

And she'd had plenty of cash. It would have been a heck of a lot easier stealing her money than forging her signature on those checks.

"So what you been up to?" Alec asked.

She wasn't about to tell him that she'd been moping around, thinking about him, or that when she closed her eyes she could feel his locks grazing her skin. She certainly wasn't about to admit that she loved him, and that he'd spoiled her for other men.

"A little of this and a little of that," she said dryly.

Alec laughed his raucous laugh. "You been partying with those fancy friends of yours. Guess what? I'm about to join their ranks."

"What do you mean?" she asked. Did that mean he was coming to Los Angeles to see her? Oh, God, her heart couldn't take that. Even as her mind processed the possibility, her traitorous body pulsed. She was getting ahead of herself. Alec didn't have money, if anyone was traveling it would be she. In two weeks she would be twenty-one and no one could stop her.

"I got the cheese," Alec said, "and from the most unexpected of places."

Cheese? Money. It took her a while to comprehend.

"Alec, you came into money?" she asked.

"Yup. My old man died and left me a fortune. I'm a millionaire, baby."

What was he smoking?

"Come again?" Maya said, slipping into the vernacular.

"I'm rich, baby, I'm rich. I'm flying out to L.A. to be with my girl."

For the second time that day she was speechless. It was

damn brazen of him to call her to tell her he was flying out to see some other girl. She should hang up on him.

"You're calling me to tell me that you're getting on a plane to visit another girl and you're expecting me to jump for joy?"

"Whoa, baby, whoa. I'm hopping a plane to see you. I got the dough and we got a couple of things to straighten out. So why waste time on the phone?"

"Alec, have you been drinking or smoking that stuff?" Maya asked.

"I'm as straight as they come. I'll tell you the whole story when I see you. I booked the best room at the Ritz. Be there tomorrow at five o'clock and wear the sexiest outfit you got."

Maya held the receiver away from her ear. A dozen questions flashed through her mind. Alec with money? "You're pulling my leg, right?" she eventually said.

"Honey, the only thing I intend to pull on is that beautiful earlobe of yours. I'm going to sink my teeth into your cinnamon flesh, and make hot, sweet love to you until you can't make hot sweet love anymore. I'm going to hold you in my arms and tell you how we're going to manage to be together."

Alec's outburst had her blushing. She wasn't sure she believed him, but if he was coming to Los Angeles she would be at the Ritz. Mentally she was already going through her closet thinking of what she would wear.

"I'll be at the hotel tomorrow," Maya said. "And you better be there."

"With bells on, baby. With bells on. I plan on showing off my sweet girl, so wear something nice."

Nice wasn't good enough. She had a treat in store for Alec. Sweet Maya planned on shaking him up.

"Come on, mamita, you can do better than that," Lourdes said. "You're going on a date, not a job interview. Show a little cleavage."

Sucking her teeth, Lourdes dismissed the little black number Vivianne held up.

"What's wrong with my dress? It's basic black, elegant."

"Basic black's blah," Lourdes said, stepping into the walk-in closet and going through the racks. She emerged with three dresses over her arm and flung them on the bed.

"Try these. You need to brighten up that brown skin. Wear something that says ravage me."

"I'm not looking to be ravaged," Vivianne cried. "The man's in town on business. We're having dinner and that's about it."

"What about after dinner?" Lourdes said pointedly. "You need to make the man sweat. Make his tongue hang out of his mouth. Get rid of that white underwear."

Vivianne sighed. Her briefs and bra were clean and that's all that was required of her. She hadn't planned on seducing Sage. She'd planned on treating their dinner as two friends meeting to renew their acquaintance.

Lourdes was digging through her dresser drawers. She found a flesh-toned strapless bra and matching bikini bottom and flung it at her. "Here, try these."

Knowing there was no point arguing, Vivianne quickly changed. She eyed Lourdes's dress selections, dismissing all of them as too risqué. Even so, maybe she should try them on.

"Let me have one."

Lourdes picked up a red halter dress and tossed it at her. "This should have the man sitting up and begging for more."

Vivianne had worn the red dress only once. She'd draped a shawl over the top, disguising its sexiness. Attempting to pacify Lourdes, she wriggled into the frock.

Lourdes circled her. "Not bad. Not bad at all."

"I'd feel more comfortable in the gold dress," Vivianne murmured.

Lourdes rolled her eyes, handing her the dress with the spaghetti straps. "Whatever you say, mamita."

The gold dress was snug, hugging all the wrong places. It complemented her coloring.

"Now shoes," Lourdes said, disappearing into Vivianne's cavernous closet again, and returning with a pair of beige slides. "You've got fifteen minutes, now move."

Fifteen minutes before she saw Sage. Fifteen minutes to fix her face and do something with her messy hair.

The doorbell rang as Vivianne slid into her backless sandals. "Oh, God, he's early," she muttered.

"I like a man who's ready to go. I'll get the door," Lourdes said, hurrying off. "Let me ply him with wine while you make yourself beautiful."

"But I still haven't decided what to wear," Vivianne cried.

"You're wearing it," Lourdes said, leaving her.

As Vivianne applied makeup, she heard Sage and Lourdes talking. It was a mistake leaving them alone. Heaven knew what Lourdes would say to him. She completed her transformation and gave a quick glance in the mirror. Not bad. Not wonderful, but not awful.

Vivianne entered the living room to find Sage and Lourdes chatting away like old friends. Lourdes had turned on the stereo and a soothing jazz tune played in the background. Spotting Vivianne, Sage jumped to his feet. Vivianne's breath caught in her throat as she faced him.

"You look terrific," Sage said, taking her into his arms and kissing her on the cheek. "Better than terrific, hot."

Viviane's entire body tingled and a flush began at the tip of her toes and slowly made its way up to her neck. She felt alive again. On fire. Sage held her away from him, his gray gaze slowly assessing her.

He was dressed in a blue jacket, cream-colored shirt, and gray slacks. His tie, a combination of blue, gray and beige, pulled it all together. She'd never seen him so formally attired. He was striking, right off the cover of *GQ*.

Lourdes cleared her throat. "What time were those dinner reservations of yours?"

"Seven."

"Seven-thirty," Sage confirmed.

"Then you need to move it. It's ten past the hour."

Sage took Vivianne's arm and guided her to the door. Over his shoulder he tossed, "Great meeting you, Lourdes. Thanks for filling me in."

Vivianne wondered what secrets Lourdes had divulged. A quick look her friend's way gave no indication. Lourdes fumbled with the knobs on the stereo, searching for a Latin station.

Outside, a charcoal-gray SUV was parked on the wrong side of the road. Sage waited until she was comfortably seated before sliding behind the wheel. He put the vehicle in gear.

"It's a rental," he offered, answering her quizzical look. "I can get back to Collins Avenue, beyond that I'm not much good."

Vivianne provided directions through the crowded streets. All traffic seemed headed for South Beach.

"The concierge at my hotel suggested The Palms, said it was the hottest place on the strip. The address is Ten Ocean Drive. Have you heard of it?"

"Can't say I have."

She wouldn't be much help. In the last few months she hadn't kept up with the goings-on in Miami.

"There's Ten Ocean Drive," Vivianne yelled as they flew by the restaurant. Sage stopped on a dime.

The building, a refurbished art deco, was a long white column. A Haitian valet accepted the SUV's keys and drove off, leaving an effusive maître d' to take over. He led them to an outside terrace and seated them under a white umbrella. Tiny white lights rimmed the railings of the balcony, providing a festive atmosphere. Those same lights adorned the umbrellas and twinkled in the trees. A salty ocean breeze tickled their nostrils and a wandering guitarist entertained requests.

"What a spectacular place," Vivianne said, looking around.

"I should have dressed more casually," Sage said, loosening his tie, "but I wanted to look nice for you."

She shuttered her eyes, enjoying the meaningless flirtation. Better to ignore it.

Wine was offered, and declined. Vivianne settled on a rum runner while Sage opted for scotch on the rocks. They clinked glasses and exchanged the requisite salutations.

"Cheers."

"Cheers."

"Mind if I get more comfortable?" Sage asked, after some time had passed.

Vivianne shook her head. "Of course I don't mind."

He lost his jacket and took off his tie. Vivianne's eyes fastened on the strong column of his neck. She was fascinated by his well-defined biceps as he pocketed the tie.

Memories of what he looked like naked surfaced. She needed to put that buff body out of her mind.

A group of young Latin women seated at a nearby table stared at Sage. Vivianne didn't need to strain her ears to overhear their conversation.

"*Dios mio,* that man is hot," one of them said, loudly.

"*Coño,* I'm boiling up."

The exchange continued in heated Spanglesh. Vivianne understood enough to realize they'd decided that Sage could park his *zapatas* under their bed any time. The graphic conversation made her blush. She'd been there, done that, and it had left her wanting not just his shoes, but his entire closet in her house.

Their waitress appeared, slapping down menus. She was young, hip, and wore an assortment of earrings. All of them shook.

"You from out of town?"

Vivianne left it for Sage to answer. After the grunge child left, she peered at him from over the top of her menu.

"Speaking of being from out of town, how long will you be here?"

"Now that depends," he answered, white teeth flashing against his mahogany skin.

Vivianne felt the familiar ping in her stomach. She needed to be careful; Sage wasn't in Miami for good.

"Depends on what?"

"You."

She felt herself getting flustered again. The ping in her stomach was now a pong.

"What do I have to do with your assignment?" she asked, playing it cool.

"Everything."

Vivianne willed her roiling stomach to settle. "Everything? You were incommunicado for weeks, now you show up in Miami telling me that your visit has something to do with me."

"It does," Sage said, reaching for her hand and pressing it slowly to his lips. "I left Venice in a hurry. I'd just found out I'd gotten my job back and there wasn't time for conversation. When I learned about this assignment, I jumped on it. I wanted to see you, Vivianne. Badly."

She was supposed to be flattered—no, honored—that he'd come to see her. And maybe she was, since her entire body throbbed.

Conscious of the women at the nearby table still gaping, Sage flashed them a porcelain grin. With a collective sigh they buried their noses in their menus and just about died. The distraction helped to lighten the moment.

"That's more like it," Sage said, noting that her lips twitched. "I like the more relaxed Vivianne Baxter on home turf."

"You like me better?" Vivianne asked, throwing caution to the wind and deliberately flirting with him.

"I won't say that. Even though you're delightful, vibrant, and sexy. There was something very appealing about caring for a vulnerable woman. Your copper-colored skin has my mouth watering, and the lower part of me is standing at full attention. Would you like to see?"

Vivianne burst out laughing as he threatened to stand. She shoved him back into his seat.

"You're just so intriguing," he said. "You have a beautiful home and eclectic furnishings that mirror your style. I'm drawn to the warm colors on your walls. I think they might mirror your soul. Are you ready to order?"

Just as she was about to reach over and kiss him, he'd changed the mood of the conversation. Sage Medino was not your typical FBI agent. No law enforcement type she knew waxed poetic like this. What did he want with her, truly want with her?

Their waitress, whose hair looked as if she'd cut and styled it in a blender, returned, took their order and left. In her absence, Sage filled Vivianne in on his reinstatement to grace, and the status of the men who'd set him up.

"The Bureau should be grateful you're not suing them," Vivianne said, her hand resting lightly on Sage's wrist.

He covered her wrist with those large hands of his. "Don't think I'm not tempted, except I have to think of my career. It would end rapidly, you know."

Vivianne thought about how hers had ended, about needing a job, and about her dwindling funds. Not tonight. She would worry tomorrow.

"Did the Italian police ever call you?" Sage asked, breaking into her meanderings.

Vivianne shook her head. "Nope. I guess it's a case of out of sight, out of mind."

"I can inquire if you'd like. The FBI has an Italian branch. I'll be happy to try."

"I'd appreciate that."

She needed that closure or she'd never feel safe. She had to assume the men in Venice had been hired by Harold Huggins. As long as they were free, anything could happen to her.

Dinner was plopped down before them, and the waitress left in a jangle of metal.

Vivianne nibbled on soft-shell crab, while Sage wolfed down oversize shrimp. She watched him gobble his food, thinking he certainly had an appetite for someone in such good shape.

Over after-dinner drinks, Sage asked, "Do you have an early morning appointment?"

"No, why?"

"Because you're coming home with me."

She gasped and made a quick recovery. "Sure of yourself, aren't you?"

"Very sure."

Vivianne threw him a lopsided grin. They'd been good together and opportunity often only knocked once. Even now, she could feel his hands on her body and smell his musky scent. She was in love with him. Why not take what he had to offer? For one night or as long as it lasted.

Vivianne watched Sage slap his credit card down. When he placed an arm around her shoulder, she snuggled next to him. It felt good to be home.

Eighteen

Sage had booked a room at The Eden Roc, a hotel that overlooked a picturesque pool. Vivianne stared out the window, admiring the way the recessed lighting provided the perfect atmosphere for the few couples strolling by.

Sage was getting them wine from the minibar. "Red or white?" he asked.

"White," Vivianne answered automatically.

Sage came to stand beside her, one arm trapping her firmly against the window casing; the other reached out and with butterfly strokes, grazed her cheek. A small tremor slithered up Vivianne's spine. Sage's manly scent invaded her nostrils.

"Great view," Sage said, looking out onto the beach and the swaying coconut trees in the distance.

"That it is."

She was conscious of his warm breath caressing her neck. It sent tiny needle pricks up her arms and made her stomach do jerky flip-flops.

"Come, sit," Sage said, his arm circling her waist and pulling her up against him.

She could feel his heat, palpable and demanding. He brought her with him to the couch, and soft pop now replaced the soothing jazz. It was music designed for dancing. Music meant for romancing.

Sage's jacket and tie hung over the arm of the sofa. He

slipped off his shoes and sprawled out, feet propped on the coffee table. "Might as well get comfortable."

Vivianne kicked off her slides and joined him, one foot carelessly placed under her butt, the other twitching its hot-pink toenails in the air.

Sage slid a glass of wine at her.

"What will you do if you can't find a job?" he asked, his long fingers circling the stem of his glass.

Vivianne shrugged. "Move, maybe."

"What about your house?" Sage asked, pointedly.

"What about it? Houses can be sold or rented."

She was careful to keep her voice even, and not let him know how much it would hurt to give up her things. She'd made up her mind that if it came down to it, moving would be what she would do.

"I've been offered a directorship," Sage said, surprising her.

She was glad for him.

"Oh, that's wonderful, especially with all you've been through. You will accept, won't you?"

"I'd be foolish not to. Every FBI agent aspires to be a director. There aren't many blacks holding that position."

"I'm proud of you," Vivianne said, leaning over to kiss his cheek, and almost spilling the wine.

"Careful," he said, setting both glasses firmly on the table and taking her hands. "Let's talk about us."

Us? There was no us. Sage was simply passing through, that was reality. She stared at him wide-eyed, waiting.

"We met at a difficult time in our lives," he said. "It's amazing that we found each other."

Sage blew a soft kiss against the sides of her mouth and she melted.

"What are you saying?" she asked, as her chest tightened and she came close to hyperventilating.

"I'm saying that we shouldn't just give up and let it go. We should explore the possibilities."

Vivianne's breath caught in her throat. What he was proposing was too much to hope for. "Y-y-you live on one coast and I on the other. It seems impossible," she stammered.

"Distance is no excuse these days," he said, drawing her closer until she came close to drowning in his cologne. "Flying isn't as expensive as it used to be. We can alternate going back and forth."

Under normal circumstances it could work, except she had no job, ergo no money. Vivianne let out a deep sigh and let her head rest on his chest. "I don't know."

"What don't you know?" Sage said, sliding the strap of her dress down one arm and using his warm mouth and moist breath to caress her flesh. Tiny noises came from the back of her throat when he unzipped her dress and tugged it down. His hands were all over her body, urgent and demanding. She unbuttoned the buttons of his shirt, slid her hands into the opening, and wove her fingers through his chest hairs.

"That feels good," Sage said.

What he was doing to her felt better. He bent his head, nibbled one nipple, and caressed the other. Tremors of want shot through her body, taking on a life of their own. When he took a nipple into his mouth, she refused to think and simply gave in to the feeling.

"Let's take this to the bedroom," Sage said against her ear.

Vivianne's legs threatened to buckle as she somehow got to her feet and let him lead her there. She was conscious of being lowered onto a firm mattress, of Sage's heavy weight settling on top of her. Somewhere along the way he'd lost his shirt and the heat of his body singed her.

Sage's fingers probed her throbbing center, unfolding the petal-soft skin and diving into the moisture. Vivianne reached for his belt buckle, fumbling to undo the notch. Helping hands aided her.

He rolled off, frantically scrambling out of his pants and

kicking them to the floor. When he came back to bed he shifted her to face him. Vivianne had the presence of mind to note that his need was a sizable knot. Her hand covered the bulge, massaging, probing, coaxing. He shoved his shorts aside so that she could have full access.

The air conditioner hummed in the background, and a popular tune came on the stereo. Vivianne forgot about everything other than the fact that her body pulsed and Sage would soon quench her thirst. His hands ravaged her breasts, titillating the flesh, and traced a path down to her stomach. His tongue was warm and moist against her back as he circled and licked. The intimacy of it all sent her hurling over the top crying his name.

"Sage."

"I'm not going to last," Sage said, sliding a condom up the length of him and settling Vivianne on top of him. "Venice was a long time ago. Hold on, baby."

But there was no holding on. She straddled him, sat back, and waited for the first thrust. When it came, her thighs clamped around his hips, and she rode him with wild abandon, putting into the motion all her pent-up need.

"We're almost there," Sage cried in a husky whisper.

His voice, the music, sent Vivianne spiraling out of control. She screamed his name again.

"Sage."

"I'm with you, baby. I'm with you."

She was with him, too, as he drove into her relentlessly, forcing her to give what she'd already given, and much, much more. Another thrust sent her off to a point of no return. Sage came with her, crying out nonsensical words. His warm liquid gushed out, filling the condom. For her, the world stood still.

Afterward, they lay staring dreamily at the ceiling until the rude jingle of a phone destroyed their peaceful mood.

"Who would be calling at this hour?" Sage groused.

"Don't pick up."

"Have to. Might be my job."

Bare-assed, he went off to investigate.

Vivianne positioned herself comfortably under the covers waiting for him to come back. He reappeared, bringing her purse with him.

"It wasn't mine, so it must be yours," he said, handing over her purse.

Puzzled, Vivianne fished out her cell phone. A message waited. She was about to retrieve it when the phone rang again. The number flashing was Lourdes's. What could her friend possibly want at that hour?

"Hi, what's up?" Vivianne said, hoping she didn't sound too annoyed.

"Thank you, *Dios,"* Lourdes rambled. "Your alarm went off. Someone broke into your home. The security company tried reaching you. They called me when they couldn't get through. The police are all over the block. *Por favor, mamita,* you need to get here quick."

"My house was robbed?" Vivianne asked, sounding stricken.

"Your house was robbed?" Sage repeated.

"I don't know if anything's missing," Lourdes cried. "Better for you to come and find out yourself."

"I'm on my way."

She looked around, searching for her clothes. While Lourdes rambled on, Sage silently handed Vivianne her clothing and got dressed quickly. She was about to race off when she realized she had no way of getting home.

"I'll take you," Sage said, car keys already in hand. "You're in no shape to face the police alone."

"Thank you."

She gave him a hug, and he held her, kissing the top of her head. "What would I do without you?" Vivianne said.

"No need to be without me," he answered. "I've already come up with a plan."

"Maya," Alec said, his eyes practically bulging out of his head. "Just look at you, babe." He twirled her around, admiring the hot-pink miniskirt that barely covered her butt and the matching chartreuse and pink halter top.

Maya had dressed carefully. She'd wanted to make a statement. She'd wanted him to sit up and notice her. Alec had put her through a lot, and needed to know she was no child to be toyed with.

Her mother had thrown her a disapproving look as she sashayed from the house. Maya had simply ignored it. She was almost twenty-one and could do anything that she wanted. No one could stop her.

Alec scooped the dreads off his face. She could tell by his actions that she made him nervous. Go figure that, cool Alec, jittery around her. Let him stew.

"You want a drink?" he asked, his voice sounding uncertain.

"A drink I could definitely use."

She followed him through the cool lobby and outside to the pool where a gaggle of her mother's friends were having drinks. They stared at her, then at Alec. She nodded at one, waved to the other, and hooked her arm through Alec's. She would be the topic of every dinner conversation tonight. She would bet on it.

Maya hitched up her skirt, showing plenty of thigh, and climbed onto the bar stool. She crossed one leg over the other. Alec looked as if he might die. His eyes were riveted on her legs and she gave him a catlike grin. He cleared his throat.

"What will you have?" he asked.

"A vodka martini, please."

It was the first grown-up drink she could think of.

"You sure? That stuff's pretty strong."

"Very sure."

Drumming his fingers against the Formica bar, he ordered the martini and a beer for himself.

"So tell me about this money you inherited," Maya said, wanting to break the uneasy silence.

Alec eyed her slyly. "Since when are you interested in money?"

"Since you inherited it," she said, giving it back.

His smile grew even more cunning. "So now I'm okay because I'm in your league and good enough to bring home to Mama and Papa?"

He'd hit a nerve. Damn him. "I was interested in you before you had a dime," she said, tossing her hair. "Your money makes no difference."

Alec bit back a snappy response when the bartender slid their drinks at them.

"Here you are. Would you like to keep a tab running?"

"Yes, keep the check open."

Grateful for the distraction, Maya tossed back half of her drink. Warmth settled in her belly, making her brave.

"Look, I didn't come to fight," she said. "I came to see you and say that I was sorry. I'm sorry we had a misunderstanding. I've missed not having you around."

"I've missed you too," Alec said, his tone softening. "Hell, Maya, things aren't the same without you in my life."

"Then why didn't you call me?" she asked, crossing and uncrossing her legs, and getting immense satisfaction from seeing how uncomfortable that made him.

Alec scratched the side of his face. "Good question. Guess I was afraid to call. You were spitting mad when you left, and nothing I said or did made a difference. I was hoping you'd cool off."

"I've cooled off," she said, draining her glass. "Get me another."

"Maya," Alec said warningly, "can you handle another martini?"

"I asked for another. I want another," she snapped. "Who appointed you my father?"

Alec signaled to the bartender to fetch them another round. His fingers stroked her bare shoulder. "I don't want to be your father, what I want to be is your lover and friend."

He'd put it out on the table. She could take what he was proposing or leave it. Except there was still one major problem: a whole continent separated them.

"You're in New York," Maya said. "How are you going to manage that?"

"I'll move if that's what it takes. I can finish school here. Set up a gallery, go back and forth, still see my mother and sister. The money I have now makes that possible."

"You'd do that for me?" Maya asked, dumbfounded that someone could care about her so much he'd willingly make a drastic change.

"I'd do that for us," Alec confirmed.

"Then what are we waiting for, boy? Take me to your room and ravish me."

Canceling their drinks, Alec signed the check with a flourish.

He held Maya's hand as she breezed by her mother's friends, smiling sweetly. They entered the elevator and got off at his floor.

Entering his suite, Maya realized the place must cost a fortune. Alec answered her silent question.

"I signed the agreement accepting my inheritance, and got an advance."

Maya was already busy stripping off her clothing. "Forget your inheritance," she said. "Don't keep me waiting." She bounced on the bed making sure everything jiggled.

The sight of her naked body galvanized Alec into action. He quickly disrobed and joined her. She would give him a treat, be the aggressor. It was a role she would enjoy to its fullest.

Maya wrapped her arms around Alec's neck, and pressed her body against his. She kissed him as he ran calloused palms across her skin and bent to capture an already taut nipple in his mouth. Her entire body sang as he continued to strum her.

Using her bare foot, she traced a path across his buttocks and let her toes linger, teasing, nudging, eliciting a response from deep within his gut. She held him in her hands, kneading his groin until he was squirming.

Maya's entire body buzzed as Alec's fingers roamed her flesh, finding all of the secret hidden spots. She gave in to the feeling, inhaling his masculine scent and responding to his urgings.

Alec rolled her onto her back and positioned himself on top of her. He reached over to the nightstand and removed a foil packet from his wallet. He parted her legs, entered her swiftly, and with an urgency that had built up, rammed into her. Alec pumped and she contracted. The momentum built, driven by a need to put any misunderstanding behind them. It came to a head as they found nirvana.

In a brief lucid moment, Maya realized that despite their different backgrounds, she and Alec shared something special: a bond that didn't require any explaining.

Nineteen

"Can I see some identification?" the uniformed cop guarding the entrance of Vivianne's house asked.

Before she could retrieve her driver's license from her bag, Sage flashed his FBI credentials.

The policeman seemed puzzled and put out. "It's only a house alarm; we don't need the FBI's help."

"I'm not on official business," Sage said, showing a flash of teeth. "I'm Ms. Baxter's date."

"Oh." The cop placed a hand on his holster as if he needed protection. You're *the* Vivianne Baxter?" He eyed Vivianne curiously.

The headlines came back to her in a rush, and feelings of shame surfaced. Her face had been splashed across every front page. The story had even made the evening news. Of course he would recognize her name. She'd been labeled a piranha, a woman who couldn't keep her hands off men, a slut.

Vivianne took a deep breath. Best to hold her head high. "Yes, I'm Vivianne Baxter, is that a problem?"

"No problem," the cop said, his cockiness slipping. "You own this house?"

"Yes, I do."

"Then you might as well go in."

Vivianne strutted into bedlam. Cops roamed around dusting for prints while a distraught Lourdes tried to answer questions as best she could.

"Thank God you're here," she said, spotting Vivianne. "I don't know if anything's been taken."

Vivianne gave a quick glance around the messy living room. The cushions of her couch were strewn on the floor and books spilled from the cases. Knickknacks had been pulled from the breakfronts and lay everywhere. At least her artwork was still on the walls. She made a mental inventory of her valuables. Her stereo was still there, and so was her television, thank God. But who knew what awaited her in her bedroom, where she kept her jewelry. How could anyone accomplish such devastation in the few minutes it had taken to sound the alarm and notify the police?

In a daze, Vivianne said to one of the cops, "I'm going to take a quick walk through and see if anything's missing." She headed for the bedroom, Sage trailing her.

Inside was the same messy state as the living room. Sheets were stripped off the bed and pillows tossed on the floor. Whoever had broken into her home had to have been looking for something, but she couldn't quite figure out what. She kept very little cash at home, and on the surface, all her valuables seem to be intact.

Vivianne approached the dresser, Sage still at her heels. She opened her jewelry box, prepared to find it empty. But everything was there. Everything plus a carefully folded note at the bottom. She grabbed it, unfolding it with some trepidation.

"What's that?" Sage asked, snatching the paper out of her hand and quickly reading it. Poker-faced, he handed it back. "You'll need to turn that over to the police."

Vivianne read the note, her stomach roiling.

I'm going to get you, bitch.

"Oh, God," she said, burying her head in her hands. She'd almost convinced herself it was over with. That she was jobless, but safe.

She didn't realize she was trembling until Sage snatched

the note back and practically yanked her from the room. She didn't remember being seated and handed a glass of water. Disoriented, she spotted Lourdes hovering. Normally excitable, she kept her emotions in check.

Sage spoke to the police. They scrutinized the note and bagged it. Vivianne felt the panic rise in her throat. She'd never felt so violated in her life. The home she loved, valued most, was no longer the peaceful sanctuary that she had created. She could no longer feel comfortable there, knowing that someone had touched her things.

"We'll need to ask a few questions," a burly policeman said, approaching and dismissing Lourdes with a nod of his head. "Ms. Baxter, do you have enemies that you know of?"

Vivianne couldn't think. Who could she have upset so badly that they would risk breaking and entering? After a moment or so, she concluded it could be any of a number of people. There had been Harold Huggins and those men who'd conspired to have her fired from WOW. There were the men in Venice, allegedly hired by an American. After she'd made headlines, a slew of hate mail had followed.

There were women claiming she'd disgraced the gender, and taken liberation too far. Men who'd said that women like her were the reason they got accused of date rape. She'd been called a number of nasty things.

Enemies? She supposed she had plenty. Vivianne began to ramble, naming names until finally Sage cut in.

"Ms. Baxter has had enough. She needs her sleep," he said, firmly.

"Okay, we're just about done," the cop answered. "Don't touch anything until we talk tomorrow."

"I can't sleep here?" Vivianne muttered, looking around the trashed room.

"You're not sleeping here," Sage said firmly, his arm linked around her waist.

"We'll increase surveillance," the cop interjected. "We'll make sure our patrol car stays on the block."

"And that's supposed to make me feel better?" Vivianne said, her lips quivering from the stress and lack of sleep.

The cop had the grace to blush. He avoided Sage's glare and quickly buried his nose in his pad.

"You'll stay with me," Sage said, stalking off to find Lourdes. "Maybe your buddy can hang out and lock up."

"Lourdes is probably more scared than me," Vivianne called after him.

"I'll talk to her. We'll see."

Whatever Sage said to Lourdes had a miraculous affect; her friend pulled herself together, and flashed a confident smile as she approached.

"Go on, *mamita,*" Lourdes said. "Get some sleep. I can handle the rest of this."

Too grateful to argue, Vivianne kissed her cheek. "I owe you, big time, hon. Him too." She managed to throw a wobbly smile Sage's way.

He came hurrying over, pulled her into his arms, and kissed her on the mouth. That one kiss hurled her over the moon and made her realize that without Sage, nothing else mattered.

Vivianne managed a grin as Sage practically carried her out.

Stan Gabriel peered over the dinner table at Alec. "Are you currently in school, young man?"

"Yes, sir."

His wife, a really turned-out older babe, sniffed and shifted her food around. She hadn't touched a scrap on her plate.

For Maya's sake, he needed to be cordial. Initially, when she'd tendered the dinner invitation, he'd politely declined.

Alec wasn't ready to meet anyone's movie star parents, even his girl's.

Now, as he faced Nona, he realized Maya was the spitting image of her mother. At least the genes were good. Maya would be beautiful well into old age. Alec still couldn't quite believe that he was sitting at the Gabriels' dinner table, sipping expensive wine and fielding an onslaught of questions.

Old man Gabriel was glaring at him, his cutlery poised. Alec wanted to sniff under his arms and see if his deodorant had failed him. Maya's parents were as far removed from his down-to-earth mom as they came. His mother didn't mind if her children helped themselves from the pot or watched television as they wolfed down their meal.

"Where do you go to school, young man?" Gabriel asked as a white maid hovered in back, holding a platter with the next course.

Alec gave Maya's father a blank look, a look that said he didn't quite comprehend what he was asking. That look was normally reserved for snotty people. *People who don't think their feces stink.* He flinched as Maya kicked him under the table.

"Answer him," she hissed.

He could do this for her, sit through this boring dinner. Truth was, he would rather be making love to her.

"I'm attending Pratt."

"The design school?"

"Yes, the design school."

"Good, at least you haven't dropped out," Maya's smartly clad mother said, her eyes inspecting his clothes.

"I don't plan on it, provided a school in Los Angeles will accept my credits."

"You're moving out West?" Nona asked, shooting a questioning look at her daughter.

"That's right, Mother. Alec is. We want to be together."

Stan cleared his throat. "Where will you be transferring to?"

"Any university that will take me."

Alec's response didn't sit well with them. Both of Maya's parents visibly gulped. They looked like they could use Tums. He knew they'd attempted to be gracious for their daughter's sake, but clearly his appearance didn't sit well with them. Both he and Maya had decided not to mention his inheritance, at least not yet.

A strained silence descended. Alec stared uneasily at the textured ivory walls and at the gigantic mahogany table that could easily seat twenty. He fiddled with the shiny cutlery that had been lined up; he didn't have a clue which to use, he'd simply aped Maya. He counted the glasses, focused his attention on the heaping platters of food with items he couldn't even guess at. His goal now was to finish his meal and get out of there. Even with the money he inherited, he would never fit in with this crowd.

"Did Maya tell you why we chose her name?" Nona asked, breaking the uncomfortable mood.

Alec shook his head. He forked up a hunk of meat and plopped it onto his plate.

"Hey, Maya, you holding out on me?"

Maya blushed and reached for his hand. He brought her palm slowly to his lips and kissed it.

Her parents gawked. Stan cleared his throat and they continued eating.

Nona's diction became more clipped as she spoke quickly.

"We wanted our daughter to have a name she was proud of. Maya Angelou is a favorite poet of ours. Her voice is renowned, her writings legendary. She's been a dancer, an actress, a professor, and an activist. She's been poor and she's been rich. And she's considered something of a prophet. She's been nominated for an Emmy, won a Grammy, and worked with Doctor King. She's planned strategy with Malcolm, fed Billie Holiday in her kitchen, and lived all over the world. All that and she's fluent in five languages. She's an inspiration to us all."

"That she is" were the only words Alec could find to say.

"And that's what we hope for Maya," Stan said. "Greatness. We carefully select the people who come into her life."

Alec was getting the message loud and clear. He wasn't good enough for their daughter. Except they were missing what he already knew. Maya was in love with him. If he got up and walked out, she'd walk too. But he would never put her in the position of choosing between him and her parents.

Alec sensed the palpable tension. Maya had gone rigid next to him. He took a calming breath and decided to make peace.

"I grew up listening to Maya Angelou's poetry," he said.

Nona and Stan gaped at him as if he had two heads.

"I have the CD she made with Ashford and Simpson. It's called *Been Found,* and it's one of my favorites. My mother thought Maya Angelou was da bomb."

"Smart woman, your mother. What does she do?" Stan asked, for the first time showing real interest.

Here was an opportunity for Alec to redeem himself. If he could produce a mother who was at least acceptable, he was in. He wasn't going to play their game. His mother was what she was. Take her, leave her. He loved her.

"My mother is a housekeeper," he said.

The maid waiting patiently behind him gasped. She covered it with a cough and continued serving.

Nona's eyes twinkled. She beamed at him. "A horticulturist, you said. Such a worthy profession."

"A housekeeper," Alec repeated. "My mother cleans houses for a living."

After an awkward silence, Stan offered an olive branch. "Housekeeping is also a worthy profession."

"More wine, please," Maya said, signaling for a maid.

The same maid who'd gasped, scurried to her side, quickly refilling the empty wineglass.

Stan laid his knife and fork down, his face taking on a serious expression.

"Look, son, we might as well give it to you straight. We had big dreams for our daughter. She's our only child. We're not sure you can make those dreams possible."

For the first time Alec understood how much they must be hurting. They'd raised their child in big, bad Hollywood and were protective of her. Now he'd appeared, ruining all their plans. He was tempted to tell them about his inheritance but that seemed so shallow; besides, if their approval was based on a few million dollars, then to hell with them

"I'm not sure I can make those dreams possible," Alec said honestly. "But I'll surely try. I love your daughter and she loves me."

"Love sometimes isn't good enough," Nona said astutely.

"Love is what we have," Maya said, rising and tossing her napkin down. "I'm really disappointed in you, Mom and Dad. This has been nothing but an interrogation, and a brutal one at that. Would you feel better if Alec told you how much he's worth?"

"Take your seat, young lady, and button your lip," Stan snapped. From the stunned expressions on Stan and Nona's faces, it seemed that Maya's outburst had been totally unexpected.

"I will not," Maya yelled back, facing both parents. "I would never have believed what snobs you are until I heard it for myself. First and foremost, although it shouldn't make any difference to you, Alec has money, quite a bit of it. Second, Dad, your father was a sharecropper who believed in you. You've told me time and again that you got lucky when you auditioned. Had you not, you would still be waiting tables out here."

The maids, used to being invisible, began noisily clearing up the dishes.

"Maya," Nona said, "hush." She approached her daughter and began massaging her shoulders in an attempt to calm her down.

"Hush, what for? You sat around this table mortifying the man I love and I'm supposed to shut up? Alec, since my parents are already upset, we might as well tell them our news." Maya looked at him expectantly.

Alec cleared his throat. He did not want to be responsible for Nona or Stan having a heart attack. He remained silent.

"Okay, I'll tell them," Maya said, breaching the uncomfortable silence. "Alec and I are moving in together."

Everyone froze, even the maids.

"What was that?" Stan asked, sounding choked. He'd heard Maya clearly the first time around.

"We're moving in together," Alec repeated. "We've already picked out our house."

"What!" Stan shouted, looking apoplectic. His wife looked as if she might die.

"We love each other," Maya said. "Don't try to stop us or we'll run off and elope."

There was a clatter of crockery as a platter fell, splintering into little pieces.

Twenty

Vivianne's eyes flickered open. She was lying in a strange bed staring at an unfamiliar ceiling, and couldn't imagine where she was. A man snored softly beside her. Not good. When a warm leg brushed her thigh, she sat up and quickly pulled the sheets up to her neck. She was naked except for the pair of black bikini panties she'd put on yesterday.

Last evening's events slowly replayed in her head. Her house had been broken into and vandalized. Sage had taken charge and then left Lourdes to take over. Shock had not settled in until she'd returned to the hotel with Sage. He'd forced a glass of wine on her; the last lucid thing she remembered was lying down almost comatose.

Vivianne pushed her way out from under the covers and entered the tiny bathroom. She washed up quickly, found a T-shirt of Sage's hanging from a peg at the back of the door, and slipped into it. Deciding she was hungry, she padded back to the sitting room, found the room service menu, and began to leaf through it. Maybe she would surprise Sage and order breakfast.

A warm breath blew against the back of her neck, causing her to jump. Sage's unshaven whiskers grazed her flesh.

"Oh, you startled me," Vivianne said, turning.

"Good morning, sweetheart. I wondered where you'd disappeared to."

"Morning," Vivianne answered, feeling herself go warm and her stomach do crazy somersaults.

Sage was wearing no shirt. His jeans were zipped halfway up, and his bare chest and partially exposed groin made vivid memories come alive. Vivianne longed to brush her hands across all that exposed flesh. She wanted to run her fingers through his chest hairs and stroke his flat stomach. Sage sat down next to her and removed the menu from her hands.

"We'll stop by the house today and see how things are going," he said, giving her a little kiss.

"Good idea. Thanks for rescuing me. I would never have made it through last evening if you hadn't been there."

"I'm taking the day off," Sage announced. "I'll call the Bureau and have one of the agents get ahold of our Venetian branch. I'm reachable by cell phone if anyone needs me."

Vivianne felt compelled to protest. She couldn't expect him to baby-sit her. "I don't want to keep you from work, I'll be fine," she said.

"I've made up my mind and that's that."

Still, Vivianne's conscience warred with her. She didn't want to keep Sage away from his job, though the truth of the matter was, she welcomed his support.

"Let's order," Sage said, returning to the menu. "I'm hungry." He began mulling over the choices, settling on the continental breakfast.

After placing their order, they waited for the meal to arrive, taking turns showering and dressing. In the middle of breakfast, Vivianne's cell phone rang. The shrill sound caused the tension to return.

"Better answer that," Sage said, when she showed no signs of moving. "Could be the police, you did give them your number last night."

The thought that the police might have information forced Vivianne to pick up the phone.

"Vivianne?" a female's voice inquired. "I'm sorry to be calling this early. Can you talk?"

Vivianne glanced at the clock on the wall. It wasn't that early, it was going on nine. What could Kathryn Samuels want with her? She'd already turned down the job, and wasn't about to be swayed.

"How are you, Kathryn?" Vivianne asked mechanically.

"Excellent. In fact, better than excellent. I have great news."

She sounded like the upbeat, take-charge woman Vivianne remembered. Vivianne waited for her to go on.

"I'm getting married," Kathryn sang. "I've tendered my resignation and I'm moving to Atlanta."

It was wonderful news. Her ex-boss was in her mid-forties and this would be a second marriage.

"Congratulations," Vivianne said, waiting.

"Thank you. My fiancé is a wonderful man. Now, back to business: you'd be the perfect person to assume my job."

Vivianne held the phone away from her ear. She was conscious of Sage, hovering protectively in the background. She was being offered a wonderful opportunity but it was too late.

"What's up?" he whispered.

She covered the mouthpiece. "I've just been offered Kathryn's job."

"Vivianne," Kathryn said, "didn't you hear me? You've got the qualifications. Everyone's in agreement, you'd be perfect. WOW needs you. Think of the visibility. Think of the pay."

She'd had enough of visibility. And yes, she had the qualifications, but no longer the enthusiasm to work for an organization that had betrayed her. But one good thing had come of it all. She'd grown strong, and she'd learned a valuable lesson: anything you said or did in the business place could be interpreted another way.

"I'll think about it. May I get back to you?" Vivianne said.

"You'll think about it? Come on, Vivianne, you can do

better than that. Where in the Miami market will you find a job offering you close to six figures?"

True, but money, much as she needed it, wasn't the primary motivating factor in this decision. She needed a fresh start in an environment that didn't hold unpleasant memories. She couldn't even live in her precious house again and feel safe. She would have to figure out what to do, and soon.

"Vivianne," Kathryn repeated, "please say yes."

"I'll sleep on it, Kathryn, and again, congratulations."

Disconnecting quickly, Vivianne stood for a moment, thinking. Unbeknownst to her, tears rained down her cheeks. Sage folded her into his arms and she laid her head against the crisp cotton of his shirt, letting the tears flow freely.

Fifteen minutes later, she'd pulled herself together. Sage made his phone calls and Vivianne washed her face. In her absence he'd called the Bureau to let them know he wouldn't be in. Then he'd called the police and told them they were on their way over.

Inside the car, Sage asked carefully, "Would you give any consideration to moving to Los Angeles?"

Vivianne's heart practically stopped. The blood roared in her ears, she must have misunderstood. She looked at him through narrowed eyes, wondering where this was going.

"Sure, I've considered moving," she said. "I have to if that's what it takes to find a job."

Sage squeezed her hand. "You don't make it easy for me, do you?"

"What exactly are you saying?"

"I'm saying that I'd like you to think of moving to Los Angeles. I twisted a lot of arms to get this assignment, and not because it was particularly interesting. I'm here in Miami because of you. I wanted to see if what we shared in Venice could be replicated. We have feelings for each other. This time we're spending together makes me realize those feelings are real."

Vivianne thought about what he'd just said. In no way had Sage committed himself. How could he think that she would move in order to explore the possibility of them as a couple? She probed further.

"So let's say I sell my house, pack up my stuff, move, and it doesn't work out?"

"Well, at least we could say we gave it a try."

Easy for him to say, but what if it didn't work? She'd be alone in a strange town with no emotional support, not even Lourdes to hold her hand. Then again, what did she have to lose? It wasn't as if there were ties binding her to Miami. Her family was in North Carolina and she was not romantically linked with anyone here. Vivianne remained in a quandary. No one in her right mind packed up her life and moved across country to be with a man who hadn't once said he loved her.

"You're asking a lot," Vivianne said, ignoring the dull ache in her heart. She knew by taking this stand she might lose him.

Sage pulled the vehicle over to the side of the road. He shoved it into park and drew her close. She was practically seated on top of him.

"I'm not given to flowery declarations," he said. "I'm a practical man. But I do know we share something special. Last night you said you would never feel safe in your home again. I'm thinking a change of locale might do you good. If I accept this directorship in Los Angeles, I'll be there for an indefinite period. I care for you, Vivianne, more than I've ever cared for any other woman, including my wife. I'd like for you to become a part of my life."

She'd like that too. And though the word *love* hadn't been mentioned, Sage had qualities that complemented her own. He was take-charge, dependable, comfortable to be with. He didn't bulldoze you into seeing things his way.

"Let's give it a try," he said, his gray gaze making her go tingly all over.

Vivianne had hoped for poetry, fanfare, bells going off. She'd wanted this to be a romantic moment.

"We'll talk about it later," she said cautiously. "Right now let's just get to the house."

Sage's face welded into an inscrutable mask. She couldn't read him. He shoved the SUV into drive and eased back onto the road.

Three hours later, they'd taken care of what business they could. The police had completed dusting for prints, and a man's lighter had been found, one she'd never seen before. Urged by Sage, Vivianne arranged for a cleaning service to come in, one that Sage insisted on paying for. The cops had said they'd call should a definite lead come in.

"Where to now?" Sage asked when they were again seated in the SUV.

"The beach," Vivianne said, thinking that a stroll down the boardwalk might do them good.

Sage's eyes lit up. "Great idea. What would Florida be without a trip to the beach?"

They parked in front of one of the hotels and headed out to the ocean. On a weekday, the beach was hardly crowded, only a handful of tourists sprawled under umbrellas, braving the summer heat. Others splashed happily in the water.

Vivianne inhaled the salty air, glad for the cloudless picture-perfect day. She was starting to relax when Sage's cell phone shrilled. The unexpected sound made her tense again. Sage muttered a curse.

"Hello," he answered gruffly, listening intently, a grim expression on his face.

"So this guy is saying that he was contracted by an American. Did he say who that might be?"

Vivianne listened openly to the conversation, guessing that she was the topic.

"Interesting. They're small-time hoods out to make a quick buck. I really appreciate you jumping on this. I'll notify the police the minute we hang up."

Once he disconnected the call, Vivianne was all over him. "What was that about?"

"One of the agents contacted the Venetian police. He speaks fluent Italian and was able to find out that the remaining men who abducted you were finally caught. They were attempting to break into a home and had no problem singing like larks. They claimed they were hired by a contact in the States and offered a small fortune to send a message to you."

"And they did their job quite well," Vivianne said, nibbling on her lower lip.

"I'm calling the cops," Sage said, already depressing the numbers. "My guess is that Harold Huggins is involved."

Vivianne rested both arms on the railing of the boardwalk and stared down at the deceptively calm sea. What had she ever done to Harold to deserve this?

"I still can't imagine why Harold would go to such lengths to discredit me," she said.

"He wanted your job. You suspected he was diverting funds and he became desperate. Fear of losing everything he had worked for made him do what he did."

She should hate the man, but she didn't. Instead she felt sorry for him. Although Harold had made her life a nightmare, some good had come of it. She would never have met Sage otherwise. Harold, on the other hand, faced a prison sentence. A criminal record would follow him for life.

Sage made the connection. "This is Sage Medino," he said, turning his attention back to the phone and repeating the information his colleague had given him. "Absolutely, Harold Huggins should be the first suspect you interrogate." Sage placed his hand over the mouthpiece. "What's the name of the guy that worked for Harold?"

"Todd Aikens."

Sage repeated the name. "Okay, we'll wait to hear from you." He ended the call.

Hand in hand, he and Vivianne strolled leisurely down the boardwalk. It was time to move on.

"Happy birthday to you, happy birthday to you," the crowd at Maya's birthday party sang.

Maya pumped her arms in the air, acknowledging everyone's good wishes. When the song ended Alec kissed her.

Stan called for a round of champagne. Formally dressed waiters and waitresses brought out glasses on silver trays. Maya's friends toasted her.

It was an elegant affair. Elegant and intimidating. Alec recognized several famous faces. Never in his life had he expected to hobnob with this group. He'd broken his own rules about not getting dressed up—skipped a tuxedo and settled for a dark Nehru-collared suit. His dreads had been tightly pulled back and secured by a leather thong. He must love Maya to run around looking like this.

The Gabriels had spared no expense for Maya's party. They'd hired two bands, one that played soft rock, one that did rap. As soon as the toasts were over, a lively crowd invaded the dance floor.

Alec loosened the buttons on his jacket and gave Maya his arm. "Come on, baby. Let's show them what dancing is about." He found a clearing and began a sensual series of gyrations. Maya followed him move for move. One by one, her friends surrounded them in a circle.

Out of the corner of his eye, Alec spotted Maya's parents. From the expression on their faces, they clearly disapproved. Too bad, why should he change his style of dancing because of a couple of wealthy, stuffy people? But they were Maya's parents, and he'd made peace with them. At least he was on civil terms with them now. The song ended and he turned Maya over to Brad, a guest he actually liked. He approached Nona.

"May I have this dance?" he asked, extending a hand.

Nona seemed surprised but took his hand. She was a pretty versatile dancer and despite her too-high heels could easily keep up with him and even manage a few complicated turns.

"You're good," Alec said, smiling at her. "You have me working up a sweat."

Nona smiled, her face lighting up. She reminded him of her daughter. "I was much better when I was younger. Now I can barely keep up with you." She fanned herself. "Whooo, it's warm."

"Then we should grab a drink and get a breath of fresh air," Alec said, leading the way to the outside terrace rimmed by colorful Japanese lanterns.

Alec got them both a drink and they wove their way through the crowd, Nona stopping at tables to chat and introduce Alec to relatives and friends.

Eventually they found seats in an out-of-the-way spot. Alec decided it was the perfect opportunity to alleviate some of Nona's fears.

"I love your daughter," he began. "Very much."

"I don't doubt that," Nona said. "I'm just concerned that you come from different worlds. Love can only go so far. Maya is used to a life of privilege. She's educated, cultured, used to getting her way. I don't want to see her hurt. What happens when the novelty of your relationship wears off?"

"Maya and I communicate on a basic level," Alec answered, taking a swig of his beer. "Yes, we're physically attracted. I might not have polish but I'm willing to learn."

Nona thought about that. She tapped his arm with a manicured hand. "I have no doubt that the money you inherited will provide her with material things, but what happens when your fundamental differences and beliefs get in the way? Maya is vulnerable."

Alec had thought about all those things as well.

"I can't give you assurances that Maya won't get hurt," he said, "but I will try my best to make this work. I don't come from a prominent family or have influential friends, but I'm hardworking, committed, and love your daughter."

"I'm glad you're realistic," Nona said, rising. "I can't pretend that you are what I wished for my daughter. But if she loves you, Stan and I will do all we can to be supportive."

She hugged Alec. Awkwardly, he hugged her back. A truce had been established between them, at least temporarily.

Nona wended her way back, stopping to acknowledge the occasional greeting.

Alec spotted Maya and hurried to her. She looked stunning in a white strapless dress and flowing silver scarf, which she wore Isadora Duncan style. Her hair had been pulled off her face and twisted into a becoming knot, and there were silver sandals on her feet.

"There you are," she said, approaching. "I got worried when you and Mother disappeared. You seem to have survived her interrogation well." She wrapped her arms around his neck and kissed him on the mouth. "Did I tell you that you're the spitting image of Eric Benet?"

Alec preened. "No, you did not. I can't wait to take you home tonight. To strip off that dress and make mad passionate love to you."

"We've got another hour to go. Then you can take me home and do with me what you will." Maya slanted him a look filled with sensual promise.

"Another hour will be agony for me," Alec said, accepting the hand Maya offered and following her back into the house.

Twenty-one

"That was the police," Sage said, disconnecting the phone. "Harold Huggins confessed to hiring those thugs in Venice. He admitted he had people break into your house and leave that note. One of them left their cigarette lighter behind."

"Harold actually confessed?" Vivianne asked.

"Yes. He thought you knew more than you did about those checks. He's one sick son of a—" A foul expletive followed. Sage punctuated his words by slamming a closed fist into his open palm.

"Sick doesn't begin to describe the man—more like evil, conniving, manipulative. The list goes on," Vivianne said.

She sat in the living room of her recently cleaned house. Sage stood above her, his jaw working. She was emotionally exhausted but at least it was over with, and a tremendous weight had been lifted off her shoulders. Vivianne's fingers worried her forehead. It had been several draining months.

Sage flopped down in the seat next to her and pulled her close. It felt good snuggling against him and having him hold her. His familiar cologne tickled her nostrils. It felt good to have him beside her.

"What I don't understand," Vivianne said, "is how Harold knew I was in Europe, and how he was able to hire those crooks."

"Didn't you tell me you kept in touch with Kathryn Samuels and that you told her about your trip abroad? In a subsequent conversation you mentioned you'd signing up with the Buena Vista tour group. What if she shared that information?"

"Anything is possible. But that still doesn't explain how Harold found out when I'd be in Venice."

"Hon," Sage chuckled, "that's pretty easy to do. You call any travel agency and inquire about Buena Vista Tours, especially those going to Europe. A couple of questions, that's all it would take. Most travel agents would be pretty happy to supply you with that information."

Given what he did, she supposed he would know. "Okay, so let's say Harold did that, it still doesn't explain how he would be able to hire small-time crooks."

"There's always the Italian mafia," Sage said laughingly. "Let's not forget there's a big operation in the States. Huggins has always hung with some pretty unsavory types. All he has to say is that he needs work done in Italy. He dangles a few bucks. Presto, it's done."

Sage made it sound so simple, and she supposed it was. She'd lived a sheltered life up until now.

"Well, at least it's over with. I don't have to worry anymore," she said, laying her head on his shoulder.

He kissed the top of her head. "The only thing you have to be concerned with now is whether you're moving to L.A. or not. I'd really like you to."

It wasn't as if she hadn't spent a restless night mulling over his proposition. It was tempting to pack up everything and start afresh, yet at the same time it was scary.

"If I do decide to move to Los Angeles," Vivianne said, "where would I live?"

Sage slanted her a gray-eyed look. "With me, of course, silly. I wouldn't ask you to move cross-country without giving that consideration."

Move in with him? Vivianne had never lived with a man, and something about that prospect didn't sit right with her, not without at least having a commitment of some type. The thought of selling her home, packing up her stuff, and moving in with Sage—all on a whim—was scary.

"Vivianne," Sage said, "I neglected to say this before, but we are extremely compatible. I was never big on career-driven women until I met you. I thought they were tough. But I saw how upset you were when your house was broken into, and I realized how vulnerable you were. I do love you, honey, with my heart and soul."

She'd longed to hear Sage say those words. His love brought with it a sense of security and drove away her fears.

"I fell in love with you in Venice," she admitted, "but a relationship seemed impossible. We were both so wounded."

"It's possible now," Sage said, kissing her and making her tingle all over. "But I'm going to wait before I ask you to become my wife and helpmate.

"Let's take it a day at a time," Vivianne responded. "I'll wait." She kissed his cheek.

"Six months," Sage said. "That's all I'm asking. If we still feel this way about each other, then there's no reason we shouldn't marry."

"Six months, then."

Their agreement was sealed with a kiss, one that left Vivianne's head spinning.

Six months later

A small group gathered on the terrace of Nona and Stan Gabriel's mansion to witness the marriage of Sage Medino and Vivianne Baxter.

Vivianne had opted not to have a huge wedding, preferring to spend the money on the house she and Sage planned on purchasing. She'd invited her family, all six of them. Now her parents and her brother and sister beamed at her proudly. Lourdes and Maya made attractive bridesmaids, and Alec and Brad Fox provided willing escorts. The recently married Kathryn Samuels and her spouse graced them with their presence, flying in from Atlanta.

Maya and Alec, whom Vivianne and Sage saw frequently, had been the ones to suggest the family home, and it was the perfect setting for the kind of festivity Vivianne had wanted. Elegant yet intimate.

Sage's entire family had come to see him married, the men's stiff stances reflecting their law enforcement background. Several of Sage's FBI buddies were also there, bringing pretty dates or wives with them. Since Alec's mother and sister were in town, Sage and Vivianne had insisted they attend. Stan and Nona Gabriel had volunteered to stand up for them. With Maya so obviously happy, they'd gotten over their annoyance with Sage.

While a rented minister read from the Bible, Vivianne found her attention drifting. She wanted this to be over soon, so that she could take her husband back to their Malibu suite and make mad passionate love to him.

It had been an interesting six months. Sage had accepted the directorship and worked long hours, though he seemed to enjoy the challenge. Vivianne had found a job counseling troubled youth. It didn't pay much, but she'd made a tidy profit from the sale of her home, and Sage's salary was more than adequate.

A gazebo trimmed in beige tulle and pink cabbage roses provided the ideal place for the ceremony. Vivianne, outfitted in an attractive champagne gown with lace trimming, looked around. Sage had rented a beige morning suit and she'd never seen him look so smart or so devastatingly handsome.

As the minister continued reading, Vivianne tried her best to focus on what he was saying.

"Dearly beloved, we are gathered to witness the marriage of Vivianne Baxter and Sage Medino. . . ."

When Sage squeezed her hand two tiny tears trickled down her cheeks. She was so happy. Had anyone told her seven months ago that she would be marrying this man she would never have believed it. Life had seemed so hopeless then.

Reality came swiftly into focus when Nona's hand grazed her face, shifting the veil on the little pillbox hat.

"Do you, Vivianne, take this man to be your lawfully wedded husband?" the minister said, peering at her over half-moon glasses.

"I do," Vivianne said as Sage softly exhaled and whispered something she didn't catch.

"And do you, Sage, promise to love and cherish this woman, till death do you part?"

"I do."

They did. If the last six months were an example, they would love each other forever and ever.

Rings were exchanged, and Sage tilted her face. He gave her a kiss that sent her reeling into second heaven. When Vivianne came up for breath she had to tell him how much she loved him.

Fingers intertwined, they emerged from the gazebo to face family and friends.

Maya and Alec were the first to offer their congratulations.

"Make sure to toss your bouquet my way," Maya said, kissing Vivianne on the cheek, then turning to embracing Sage. "Be sure to treat her good."

"I get the garter," Alec said, whispering it loudly enough for Maya to hear. He took Vivianne off to the side. "As soon as Maya and I graduate, I plan on marrying her. I hope you and Sage will stand up for us."

"Oh, Alec, that's wonderful," Vivianne said, hugging him. "I'm happy for both of you. Are you enjoying the money you inherited?"

"I'm enjoying Maya more," Alec said, truthfully.

The joy of having a life partner had toned down his cockiness. He seemed comfortable with himself and much more self-assured.

Come fall, four people's lives had changed drastically. They'd been blessed with an incredible and rare gift, the gift of love.

No man could break that asunder.

Dear Reader,

Venice is truly the most romantic city in the world. There is an indescribable beauty and tranquillity to it that makes even the most hyper person relax.

Venice would be my city of choice for a second honeymoon. Picture old architecture, mysterious alleyways and side streets, wide canals, gondolas and gondoliers, and all that fabulous food.

This is the setting of Sage Medino and Vivianne Baxter's story, a story I hope you found filled with both love and intrigue.

I hope you enjoyed the beautiful setting and a suspenseful love story. To contact me with your comments, please do so at MKinggambl@aol.com. You may also write to me at:

P.O. Box 25143
Tamarac, FL 33320

Have a blessed day.

Marcia King-Gamble
www.lovemarcia.com

ABOUT THE AUTHOR

Marcia King-Gamble is a Caribbean American author and a self-proclaimed globe-trotter. "There are very few places in the world I haven't seen," Marcia admits. She's had colorful careers in the travel industry and currently makes Florida home. She admits to having a menagerie of animals, won't miss her aerobic step classes for the world, and has a wicked sense of humor. One of her favorite things to do on weekends is to attend estate sales and buy lots of stuff. She loves hearing from her fans. You may contact her at Mkinggambl@aol.com.